Other Books in the Keystone Stables Series

Summer Camp Adventure

BOOK 4

KEYSTONE
Stables

Formerly titled *Teamwork at Camp Tioga*

..... Marsha Hubler .....

ZONDERkidz

ZONDERVAN.com/
AUTHORTRACKER
follow your favorite authors

We want to hear from you. Please send your comments
about this book to us in care of zreview@zondervan.com. Thank you.

Zonderkidz

Summer Camp Adventure
Formerly titled *Teamwork at Camp Tioga*
Copyright © 2005, 2009 by Marsha Hubler

Requests for information should be addressed to:
Zonderkidz, *Grand Rapids, MI 49530*

Library of Congress Cataloging-in-Publication Data

Hubler, Marsha, 1947-
   [Teamwork at Camp Tioga]
   Summer camp adventure / by Marsha Hubler.
      p. cm. — (Keystone Stables ; bk. 4)
   Summary: Having taken a crash course in American Sign Language, Camp
Tioga junior counselor Skye tries to communicate with a troublesome camper
who is deaf, and when he disappears on horseback into the hills, she and Chad
lead the rescue team.
   ISBN 978-0-310-71795-9 (softcover)
   [1. Camps—Fiction. 2. Behavior—Fiction. 3. Deaf—Fiction. 4. People
with disabilities—Fiction. 5. Horses—Fiction. 6. Christian life—Fiction.
7. Pennsylvania—Fiction.] I. Title.
   PZ7.H86325Su 2009
   [Fic]—dc22   2009005603

Interior illustrator: Lyn Boyer
Interior design and composition: Carlos Estrada and Sherri L. Hoffman

Printed in the United States of America

12 13 14 15 16 /DCI/ 22 21 20 19 18 17 16 15 14 13 12 11 10 9 8 7 6 5 4

*Dedicated to the Bill Rice Ranch
in Murfreesboro, Tennessee*

Map of Camp Oneega

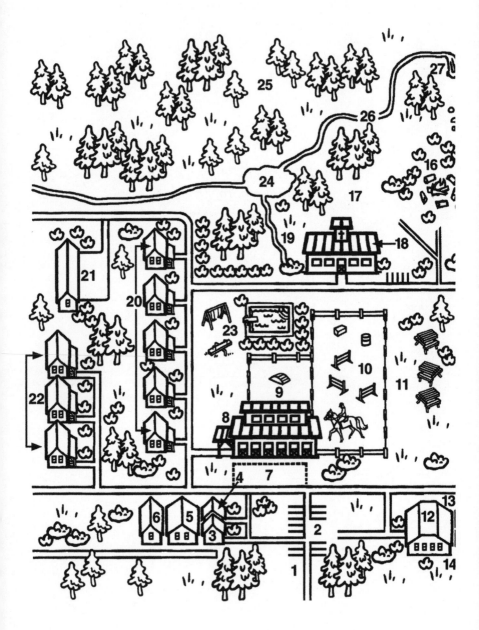

1. Entrance to Camp Oneega
2. Parking for visitors
3. Registration for campers
4. Post office
5. Country store
6. First aid
7. Loading/unloading for horse trailers
8. Barn
9. Small Paddock
10. Large corral
11. Picnic area
12. Mess hall
13. Kitchen
14. Storage
15. Girls' bunkhouses
16. Campfire site
17. Open field for relays/games
18. Chapel/all-purpose room
19. Water slide
20. Boys' bunkhouses
21. Garage/maintenance
22. Staff housing
23. Swimming pool/playground area
24. Lake Oneega
25. Shamokin State Park
26. Cherokee Creek
27. Oneega Falls
28. Secret campsite

W e're finally here!" Skye yelled, jumping out of the truck cab. Her dark brown eyes darted back and forth at the surroundings as fast as her heart was pounding. She ran both hands through her hair, nervously pushing back the long dark strands. "Morgan, I can't believe it! Camp Oneega all summer long!"

Mr. and Mrs. Chambers quickly slipped out of the truck and set up Morgan in her Jazzy wheelchair on a cement walkway.

"My nerves are frazzled, and we just got here!" Morgan giggled. "Do you think not being able to sleep for a week has anything to do with it?"

"You girls are in for the treat of your life," Mr. Chambers said. He squared his cowboy hat on his brown hair and smoothed his mustache.

"You certainly are!" Mrs. Chambers smiled all the way to her blue eyes. "We're very proud of our foster girls volunteering to be junior counselors and riding instructors. Since you both have experience with horses and with special-needs children, you're just the teen workers this Christian camp was looking for."

"It's so cool that our church decided to send monthly support to this place," Morgan said. Her long, kinky red hair framed a freckled face upturned to the hot June sun. "After Mr. Wheaten spoke to the youth group in Sunday school last January, Pastor Newman really got sold on this place. Thanks to those two, we're here!"

Skye's attention shifted to the barn and riding corral straight ahead. "I just can't believe that serving the Lord could ever be like this. I mean, like, Morgan and me together in the same bunkhouse! And on top of that, Champ and Blaze could come too." She glanced at the trailer hooked to the back of their truck.

Neigh-h-h! At the mention of his name, the sorrel Quarter Horse whinnied and pawed the trailer floor. Blaze nickered.

"Mr. Wheaten should be somewhere close by," Mr. Chambers said. "He told us to be here by four o'clock."

"Did I hear my name?" a man's voice called from inside the barn. A large door slid open, and a giant of a man walked out with a belly that looked like he had swallowed a watermelon—whole. From the top of his cowboy hat to the bottoms of his boots, he was covered in hay dust. He banged his black Stetson on his jeans, wiped his sweating face on his sleeve, and squared the hat on his silver crew cut. "Whew! Sure is a hot one today," he said. "Stackin' hay in heat like this is worse than tryin' to catch a greased pig in a tub o' sticky oatmeal. It's almost as hot here as it was in Texas. How are you folks doin' today?" He extended his right hand to Mr. Chambers.

"We're fine," Mr. Chambers said with a warm handshake.

"Jumpin' out of our skin would be a better way to describe Morgan and me," Skye said. "We can't wait to start our jobs." *And see Chad*, she mused.

"Morgan Hendricks and Skye Nicholson, reporting for duty, sir!" Morgan said, saluting. She shook Mr. Wheaten's hand and then pivoted her chair toward a large building to her right. "I am so into cooking these days. I want to get my hands on that neat equipment in your mess hall where I'm going to spend three days each week. At home I even practiced making brown bread and black-eyed peas."

"Yeah," Skye said, opening her mouth and pointing at her tongue. "Enough to gag a maggot."

"Skye—" Mrs. Chambers shook her head.

"Sorry," Skye said.

"Little lady," Mr. Wheaten said, "you must've been using *Charleston's Summer Cookbook* or somethin' left over from the Civil War! This is Camp Oneega, not Camp Atlanta. Pennsylvanians don't eat black-eyed peas—or grits—even if that's all that's left on the shelf. We'd rather eat wallpaper." He laughed and his watermelon belly bounced like it was dancing.

"Oops," Morgan said, placing her hand over her mouth. "I thought all camps had steady diets of grits and stuff like that."

"In these Pocono Mountains, you'll find baked beans, griddle-fried potatoes, and homemade biscuits. No grits! I repeat, no grits! Just give me a good ol' quarter-pounder nestled between two slices of fresh-baked bread, and I'm a happy camper. We've got great cooks and great eats here at the camp. I'm sure you'll be a tremendous help to our kitchen staff, little lady."

"I can't wait," Morgan said.

"Now, folks," Mr. Wheaten said, "the first thing we need to do is get your mounts bedded down and get you girls registered at headquarters." He pointed to another large building nearby. "That's your first stop. Then we'll show you your assigned bunkhouse, and after chow, you'll get the nickel tour of the place. Tomorrow the campers arrive, and we're off into a summer of 'what will happen next?' So if Annie Oakley wants to help me, we'll unload—oh—what are the horses' names?"

11

"Champ and Blaze," Morgan said.

Mr. Wheaten continued, "Okay, we'll unload Champ and Blaze so they can take a nice long nap in their stalls before munch time."

"Annie Oakley?" Skye said, scratching her head.

Mrs. Chambers laughed. "Skye, you're a little too young to know about that TV program. As a matter of fact, I wasn't around then either, but my mother told me about it because she was as crazy about horses as we are. Annie Oakley was an expert horsewoman and sharp-shooter who always wore pigtails."

"Little lady, you'd look just like her if you had pig-tails," Mr. Wheaten said. "And I am old enough to remember that TV show. One of my all-time favorites."

"Hey," Morgan said, "I learned about Annie Oakley in history class. She was a real person back in the early 1900s. Skye, you'd look cool with pigtails."

"I'll pray about it," Skye joked, walking toward the back of the horse trailer.

"Hey, burgers and cheese, but no black-eyed peas!" Skye and Morgan sang and giggled outside the mess hall after supper.

Following their introduction to "camp grub," they sat through a not-too-boring orientation with all the other volunteers. Next—as soon as Mr. Wheaten could join them—they would get their guided tour.

"I wonder where Chad is." Skye surveyed the surroundings, hoping to see a blond head and gorgeous brown eyes pop out from behind a tree. "I mean, my summer will be totally ruined if he doesn't show up. I sure hope he didn't change his mind."

Morgan wheeled down off the mess hall ramp and faced the entrance of the camp. "If I know Chad, he's

12

probably working late at the hardware store to try to get the very last buck he can earn. After all, taking a summer off to volunteer here isn't gonna help his college fund at all."

"Oh, he told me he'll get paid since he's the camp's junior activity director and the lifeguard. The pay isn't much, but at least it's something."

"I bet he'll pop his cute little dimples in here any sec," Morgan assured Skye. "And besides, don't forget why you're here. It's not exactly for making goo-goo eyes at Chad."

As the girls giggled, Mr. Wheaten came out of the mess hall. Three other teens trailed behind him.

"Well, little ladies," he bellowed, "how was your first camp chow? Morgan, if your heart's really set on black-eyed peas, I'll run into town to the store and get you a can." He roared with laughter.

"I'll pass." Morgan laughed too.

Mr. Wheaten waved at the teens coming along behind. "C'mere, kids. I want you to meet some of your co-workers."

They lined up beside the man.

"Skye and Morgan," he began, "this is Tim Marshall, Caleb Grant, and Linda Kraft."

The teens exchanged hellos.

Mr. Wheaten continued, "Tim is part of the barn crew. He'll be workin' with the horses, so you two will see a lot of him. Caleb's helping out the grounds crew and maintenance, and Linda is our lifeguard."

"Lifeguard?" Skye's tone sounded defensive. "I thought Chad Dressler was the lifeguard, I mean—"

"He can't be on duty every hour every day," Linda said as if she were correcting a toddler. "The poor guy would turn into a lobster—even with an umbrella over him."

Well, whoop dee doo, Skye thought. She stared pitchforks at Linda's golden curls, sky-blue eyes, and dimples.

And you better stay away from him. "Chad *is* coming, isn't he, Mr. Wheaten?"

Mr. Wheaten smiled. "Yeah, he should be here early tomorrow morning. He had to put in double time on his last day of work."

Skye glanced at Morgan, who shot her an I-told-you-so smile.

"Speaking of working," Caleb said as he started walking away, "they want me over at the garage. Something about greasin' lawn tractor axles and pumpin' air into tires. See you guys later."

"Okay, Caleb." Mr. Wheaten turned toward Skye. "Anyway, just as you've done, Tim and Linda have taken a crash course in American Sign Language. Tim is the chaperone in the boys' bunkhouse where Jonathan Martin will be staying. Jonathan's the only hearing-impaired camper we have this year. We always plan to have at least two deaf children, but the other deaf boy who wanted to come had to have his tonsils out last week. Jonathan's parents decided to send Jonathan anyway. They told me he's used to being alone. He's only eight, he hates girls, and I hear he's a rascal."

"Does he speak?" Skye asked. "I learned in my signing class that many deaf children learn to talk."

"No, I don't think he can. His paperwork didn't say anything about that," Mr. Wheaten said. "Also, he's been signing his whole life. He won't wait for you to decipher what he's trying to say. So I'd like you to be real sharp with your signing. Maybe on some of your time off, the three of you could get together and practice. "

Tim and I will, Skye decided without a second thought. "Yeah, sure," she said.

Mr. Wheaten removed his Stetson, wiped his sweaty brow on his arm, and squared his hat on his head. "My wife knows how to sign too. She does all the chapel services, so we've got our bases covered there. But with all his different activities, Jonathan will be spending most of his time with you kids. I'm so thankful you three took the time to learn how to sign. I don't know what we could have planned for him without you."

"I guess your wife would've had to come to camp all day every day!" Tim laughed.

Mr. Wheaten joined in the laughter. "Well, let me tell you a little secret. Swimming she can handle, but horseback riding? All I can picture is a horse runnin' over the hill with a lady hangin' on for dear life."

Everyone laughed but Skye, who folded her arms and forced out a smile.

"Enough of this nonsense!" Mr. Wheaten managed to say between chuckles. "Are you kids ready for the nickel tour of this place?"

"Yeah," Skye said.

"Let's go for it," Tim agreed.

"Okay," Mr. Wheaten said, pointing across the road. "Let's start with the barn and riding corral. I need to introduce you to the horses and fill you in on the very special training each has."

The group followed Mr. Wheaten as he started across the road.

"Camp Oneega is a very special place," the man started, rambling like a real estate broker offering the deal of the century. "Now, notice that everywhere you look there are paved sidewalks, little road signs with Braille directions, ramps and stainless steel railings—but no steps. By this time tomorrow, this place will be crawling with wheelchairs, kids in helmets, guide dogs—"

"This place is so cool," Skye whispered to Morgan. "But tomorrow it will be better. Much better!"

chapter two

Skye and Morgan sat in the mess hall at 8:00 a.m. with Tim, Caleb, and all the other workers and volunteers. The large room buzzed with chatter and utensils clanging on dishes at every table. The smell of fried potatoes, toast, and coffee filled the room.

Just to see Mr. Wheaten's reaction, Skye had put on her western horse show outfit and plaited her hair into pigtails. She looked sharp in her plaid shirt, suede cowboy hat, red scarf, and leather chaps. Now she and Morgan were sampling their first taste of creamed eggs and waiting for Mr. Wheaten to come in and make the morning announcements.

"Mr. Wheaten didn't tell us about creamed eggs," Skye said out of the side of her mouth. "But I guess they're better than nothing."

"Well, they're interesting," Morgan replied. "Yeah, that's a good word for them. Interesting. They oughta call them squashed eggs, not creamed. Just wait until I get back in that kitchen, Skye. You'll think you're in food heaven. I start today after we get all our campers registered and settled in the bunkhouse."

Skye took a bite of toast and washed it down with orange juice. "Didn't Mr. Wheaten say that most of the campers will get here this afternoon?"

"Yeah," Tim said, brushing his hand over his dark brown spiked hair. His hazel eyes sparkled with excitement. "They said in registration that they're expecting 110 junior campers this week—all between the ages of eight and twelve. The place will be crawling with kids. What gets me are the ones that are scared out of their pants by horses. But I guess that's why we're here—to help our fellow man! Hey, speakin' of horses, Skye, I like your cool duds—and your hair. Are you in a skit or something?"

"Nah," Skye said. "I'm just kind of pulling a joke on Mr. Wheaten."

"How's that?" Caleb scooped up a forkful of home fries while riveting his jade green eyes on Morgan.

Skye couldn't help notice Morgan staring back. "Yesterday Mr. Wheaten called me Annie Oakley," Skye said, giggling, "and he said I'd look just like her if I had pigtails."

"And Skye's not likely to let anything like that pass without making a statement, even if it might be ridiculous," Morgan added, still staring at Caleb.

Well, well, well, dear sis, I do believe you're blushing, Skye thought as she watched the action out of the corner of her eye. *What do we have here?*

"Oh, I get it," Tim said. "Annie Oakley was some cowgirl dude who lived at the turn of the last century. Right?"

"Close enough." Morgan's attention was glued to Caleb.

Caleb stood and picked up his tray, his muscular frame bulging under his blue maintenance shirt. "Morgan, I'd like to hear more about how you ride horses even with your cerebral palsy. That's so awesome. But right now I gotta get over to the garage. How about later—like after supper?"

"Well—I—" Morgan began, blushing a shade of red that almost outdid her hair.

"She'd be glad to," Skye answered for her. "She'll have a free hour between mess hall duty and bedding down the campers, won't you?" Skye gave Morgan an only-girls-know-what-this-means smirk.

"Yeah, I guess I will," Morgan said, glancing down at her tray.

"Well, I'll see you at the bonfire then," Caleb said.

"Bonfire?" Morgan said, looking at Caleb again.

"Mr. Wheaten will tell you about it in his announcements," Caleb yelled back over his shoulder as he walked toward the tray deposit across the room.

"And how 'bout you, Skye?" Tim finally had the chance to speak. "Are you free at all today? I'd like to meet Champ. I've heard he's quite a horse. This is my third year here, so I'd be glad to tell you all about the ten camp horses. And I'll introduce you to my Appaloosa, Wampum."

"Well—I—" Skye stammered.

"She'd be glad to," Morgan piped in.

"Attention, ladies and germs," Mr. Wheaten's voice echoed from a platform at the end of the mess hall. He held up a bunch of papers and rested a microphone on his watermelon belly. "I have a list of about a million announcements for you workers and volunteers. It should only take until midnight."

The room filled with laughter.

"Seriously," he continued, "I need to review some last-minute changes in scheduling, camper sleeping assignments, and most important, the big goin's-on for the day—a get-acquainted bonfire at 8:00 p.m. tonight."

For the next fifteen minutes, Mr. Wheaten read from his papers, calling out volunteers' names and listing their responsibilities. "And last, but not least, concerning riding assignments, right after I'm done here I'd like to speak to Tim Marshall and Skye Nicholson. Tim, I saw you on my way in here, but where's Skye?" The man cupped his hand over his eyes and searched the room.

"Annie Oakley's back here!" Tim yelled, grinning mischievously. He stood and pointed across the table to Skye.

"Where are you, Annie?" Mr. Wheaten said.

Skye stood and faced the man. "Back here, Mr. Wheaten."

"Well, be still my achin' heart. If that ain't Annie Oakley in the flesh, pigtails and all!" Mr. Wheaten said. The room filled with chuckles. "Folks, all I can tell you is that our horses are gonna have the best care they've ever had with this little lady here this summer. Annie, I understand you're a blue ribbon winner in horse shows."

"Yep!" Skye yelled out as she sat. "But my horse won them. I didn't!"

More laughter erupted.

"Well, that's fantastic," Mr. Wheaten said. "I guess that just about wraps up the announcements." He glanced at the papers. "Oh, one more thing. I need to meet with my junior activity director, Chad Dressler. Does anyone know if he got here yet?"

"Reporting for duty, sir!" a familiar voice shouted from the doorway in the back of the room.

Skye spun anxiously toward the voice, smiling from pigtail to pigtail. *Be still my aching heart!* she told herself.

There in the doorway stood Skye Nicholson's heartthrob in all of his blond glory—and Linda Kraft in hers!

chapter three

All day Skye and Morgan helped their eleven campers settle into the bunkhouse, the Five Ferns cabin. As busy as Skye was, she found herself getting angrier by the minute every time she thought about Chad—and Linda.

"Lighten up!" Morgan said when Skye mentioned it during a break in the action. "It's not like you and Chad are an item or anything. He and Linda are probably just discussing rules and regs since they're lifeguardin' together. Hey, we're here to serve God and others. Keep focused!"

Skye knew Morgan was right. She had many more important things to think about. But Chad with another girl? Skye felt like a hay baler was running through her chest and tearing her heart to shreds.

It was eight o'clock in the evening, and the cool mountain air had teased the campers into sweatshirts for the get-acquainted celebration. Morgan led the children from Five Ferns down a railed sidewalk toward the open field where the small bonfire was already crackling.

Behind her trailed three girls in wheelchairs, two blind girls with guide dogs, and six other girls who were physically or mentally challenged (two wearing helmets). Skye brought up the rear as the procession made its way onto an asphalt circle.

Down several other sidewalks a molasses flow of children came, joining dozens already surrounding the fire at a safe distance. Morgan stopped at her assigned place, instructing the blind campers to line up beside her. While Skye was helping the rest of her campers do the same, someone tapped her on the shoulder.

"Hey, Skye, what's happenin'?" a familiar voice said.

Skye jumped like she had been struck by lightning. The last person she had expected to see here was Chad! "Nothing!" she said like she was a finalist in the Camp Oneega Miss Snoot Contest. She elaborately positioned one of her campers' wheelchairs into a spot where it had already been positioned. Watching Chad out of the corner of her eye, she kept herself extremely busy.

"Did you bring your violin?" Chad asked, moving into Skye's full view. "I have my guitar! Mr. Wheaten said he needs all the help he can get for this chorus and crazy-tune sing-along." He strummed an imaginary chord.

"Yes, I have it!" Skye barked. "I'll be playing for chapel services with the youth praise band. Now if you'll excuse me, I'm busy."

"Oh—yeah—sure—sorry." Disappointment and confusion filled Chad's voice. "How about a soda after the bonfire?"

"I'm busy! Morgan and I *do* have jobs here, you know."

"Yeah, I know. I'll look for you at staff devotions later then."

Don't bother, Skye felt like saying. "Mary, be careful there!" she said, ignoring Chad as she stepped around him and reached for one of the campers. "Put your hands on the railing so you don't fall. That's good."

"Okay, later." A bewildered look covered Chad's face as he walked away.

"What was that all about?" Morgan said.

"Oh, nothing," Skye snapped, watching Chad join Mr. Wheaten. "I'm focusing—just focusing!"

"Have you met Jonathan yet?"

"No, but I'm hoping to right now. Do you see Tim anywhere?"

Skye glanced around. "He should be with Jonathan."

"Nope, I don't see Tim—but there's Linda—with Mr. Wheaten and Chad. Remember, she knows how to sign too. Maybe she's already met the kid, and she could tell you where he is."

"Well, it's obvious she's not doing her job or she'd be with Jonathan—or with her own cabin kids," Skye muttered. "Seems like she can't get enough of Chad."

"Skye, cool it!" Morgan said. "Hey, over there! On the other side of the bonfire! I see Tim. Looks like he's in the middle of something goin' on that shouldn't be goin' on. Listen to the kids yelling."

Skye's glance shot to the other side of the circle. Mr. Wheaten was already running toward the rumpus.

"Morgan, will you be okay here with our kids?" Skye asked, heading toward the trouble. "Something tells me Jonathan's right in the middle of that mess, whatever it is."

"We're fine, Skye! And there are other staff members close by. We'll be cool, won't we, kids?"

"Yeah! No problem!" echoed down the line.

Skye tore around the circle to the commotion where a crowd had now formed. She struggled her way through a sea of bobbing heads to see what was happening.

"All right, that's enough!" Mr. Wheaten yelled.

Tim had his arms wrapped around a peanut of a boy who was kicking, flailing his arms, and screaming at the top of his lungs. A line of staff members was keeping the other campers out of harm's way.

Mr. Wheaten used his powerful frame to pin the boy's arms down in a bear hug. "Tim, can you get hold of his legs? Just wrap around them like I did his arms. We've got to get him calmed down. We'll carry him back there to the picnic area. The rest of you staff members, get your kids singing choruses." Mr. Wheaten looked up and saw Skye right in front of him. "Good, Skye—you're here. This is Jonathan. Sign that we're not going to hurt him—and you come with us to the picnic grove. Your signing will help while we're trying to quiet him down."

Skye mentally flipped through the pages of signs she had learned in her course last winter. She raised her hands and began, "Stop! They won't hurt you."

Jonathan studied Skye's hands and then stuck out his tongue. Again, he started flailing and screaming while Mr. Wheaten and Tim used all their strength to carry him away. Skye followed as they hurried to the picnic grove. Finally, after being plunked down at a picnic table, he calmed down. No one was there to watch him perform. Tim sat exhausted on one side of the boy, and Mr. Wheaten, puffing and sweating profusely, sat on the other.

"He was throwing firecrackers into the bonfire," Tim said, puffing. "When I searched his pockets and took them from him, he went nuts!"

"I told you he was a rascal," Mr. Wheaten said. "Skye, ask him if he's all right."

"Are you okay?" she signed.

In the distance at the bonfire, the campers started singing, "The ants come marching two by two, hoorah, hoorah—" and another lightning bolt hit Skye. *Jonathan can't hear that. He can't hear anything!*

"My neck hurts," Jonathan signed. Big crocodile tears filled his brown eyes and trickled down his cheeks, which were now beaming fire red. Drops of sweat ran from his dark curly hair and down the sides of his thin face.

Skye knelt in front of the boy, touching him gently on his knee. "We'll help you," she signed.

Mr. Wheaten stood and Jonathan flinched. "We better have him checked out at the sick bay," the man said. "I think he takes meds regularly. I want to see when he had his last dose. Skye, tell him to come with Tim and me. Tim, you can sign while we're over there. We'll leave him with the nurse, and Skye, will you go for him in about a half hour? Even though he hates girls, I'm hopin' he'll come back with you."

"Sure," Skye said and then signed to the boy, "They'll take you now to First Aid to see if there's something wrong with your neck."

"Okay," Jonathan signed then wiped his eyes with both hands.

"Oh—Skye—tell him your name," Mr. Wheaten said. "He knows who we are. He met us when he registered. It seems that he likes our Annie Oakley."

Skye tapped Jonathan on the arm to get his attention. "My name is S-k-y-e," she signed. "What's your name?"

The boy took several choppy breaths, wiped his nose on his arm, and smiled, showing a mouthful of beautiful white teeth. "J-o-n-a-t-h-a-n," he spelled and then added, "I like you. I like your stupid pigtails. You're not like other dumb girls."

"What'd he say?" Mr. Wheaten asked.

Skye felt her face flush hot. "He spelled his name—and—he said he likes me—and my stupid pigtails."

"Well, Annie, it looks like you've got yourself another fan, and that's super," Mr. Wheaten said. "If we have someone around here he likes, he might be more inclined to behave. Tim, are you ready? Skye, remember, in about a half hour, go get Jonathan at First Aid and bring him back to the bonfire."

"Will do," Skye said, smiling at Jonathan, who was still smiling back.

Tim stood, tapped Jonathan on the shoulder, and signed, "We'll go now. Okay?"

"Okay," Jonathan signed, standing. The three walked toward the sick bay, and Skye headed back to the bonfire.

After a half hour of camp tunes, choruses, and a zillion hellos with other campers, Skye headed to First Aid, which was located in the registration building. The setting sun filled the sky with rippled scales of pink and blue, and the evening mountain air had become cooler. She paused a moment to admire the beauty of God's creation before stepping into the office. It was empty, so she walked to a door labeled "Nurse's Station" and knocked.

"Yes," a hefty dark-skinned woman in a white uniform said, opening the door. Her name tag read MRS. BENNETT. "May I help you?"

"I'm Skye Nicholson, and I'm here for Jonathan Martin," Skye said.

The nurse rushed out into the office area. "But—we—I wrote on a piece of paper for him to stay right here until you came. Wasn't he sitting in here?" The panic on her face charged through Skye's veins like ice water.

"No, he wasn't," Skye said.

The nurse rushed outside and stood on the ramp, her eyes scanning the grounds to the left and right. "Oh, dear, I should have kept him in the back with me. I don't see him anywhere. I sure hope he didn't take off toward the main highway. I'll drive out to the entrance, just to make sure." She ran down the ramp, looked around both sides of the building, and ran back up. "Is Mr. Wheaten at the bonfire yet?"

"Yes," Skye said and gulped.

"Run back and tell him we've got an AWOK!"

"AWOK?" Skye started down the ramp and looked back, puzzled.

"Absent Without Our Knowledge—and hurry!"

onathan! Jonathan!" Frantic with fear, Skye started
running back toward the campfire. *Oh, that's right!
Jonathan can't hear!* She crossed the road and, when
passing the barn, noticed the door was open wide.

"That's strange!" she said, unaware that she was
having a conversation with herself. "I remember Mr.
Wheaten saying the door should always be closed tight."
Skye ran to the barn and started to slide the door shut.
What's that strange noise coming from inside? she asked
herself, standing perfectly still.

A string of timid sniffles and muffled sobs filtered to
the outside.

She peeked inside.

There in the shadows, Jonathan slumped against a
small stack of hay bales. With his elbows on his knees,
hands on his ears, and head bent low, he whimpered like
a lost puppy.

Be careful. Don't scare him, Skye thought. Stepping
inside, she dropped to her knees and crawled right in
front of Jonathan. He had no idea she was there.

Skye reached out, gently touching Jonathan's arm.

Jumping like he had been poked with a branding iron, his head shot up, and his small body recoiled tighter against the hay. Skye was startled too, but by the fear in the boy's eyes.

"Don't be afraid," Skye signed. "I'm here to help you."

What could he be so afraid of? Skye wondered. *I guess when you can't hear, a lot of things might scare you.* Suddenly she remembered Mrs. Bennett. *Yikes! She's about to start a five-county search for him.* "Wait right here!" Skye signed to the boy.

Jonathan relaxed into the hay, and a tentative smile replaced the look of panic. He brushed away the tears, wiped his runny nose on his arm, and signed, "Okay."

Skye rushed to the doorway. "I've got to find Mrs. Bennett," she said with only the barn walls listening. Just as Skye stepped outside, the nurse came rushing out from First Aid, down the ramp, and toward the parking lot. Keys dangled in her frantic hands as she raced toward her car.

"Mrs. Bennett!" Yelling and waving, Skye ran toward the woman. "Mrs. Bennett! Jonathan's all right! He's in the barn! I'll take him back to his group!" The woman spun around, and Skye stopped on her side of the road. "Everything's okay. I've got him!"

"Thank the Lord!" Mrs. Bennett let out a sigh of relief. "That child gave me one good scare. Thanks, Skye, and don't let him out of your sight for one minute." The woman turned, took a deep relaxing breath, and headed back to her station.

Skye hurried back inside the barn. Jonathan sat waiting with his legs crossed and arms folded. Now his face beamed a full-toothed smile. "I like you," he signed.

Again, Skye dropped to her knees in front of the boy. "Why were you crying?"

His skinny shoulders gave just a hint of a shrug, and his lips wrinkled into an I-don't-know gesture. "I like horses too." He pointed at the stalls.

"Would you like to see my horse?"

"Yes. Where is it?" Jonathan stood, his tearstained face fading behind a brilliant smile.

"Champ's back there in the last stall on that side. Come on, I'll show you."

✿ ✿ ✿

The next morning at breakfast, Skye studied Chad—and Linda—sitting across the room with Linda's cabin kids, laughing up a storm. Skye and Morgan sat with the Five Ferns kids, laughing up their own storm. *Not that I care one iota*, Skye thought, *but he could wave just once.*

After breakfast, Skye and Morgan lined up their kids outside the mess hall. Just then, Tim came out, leading his own group. "Hey, Skye, are you ready to teach your first riding lesson?" he said. "The sun's splittin' the skies, so to beat the heat, our lessons need to be done by noon. Mr. Wheaten gave you a schedule, didn't he?"

"Yeah," Skye said. "I need to take my campers to their assigned activities, and then I'll see you at the barn. It looks like I'll be starting with 'The Rascal.'" She pointed to a youngster standing behind Tim.

"The Rascal?"

"Yeah, your friend and mine, Jonathan Martin. He's my first rider.

"Hey, you're definitely starting out with a bang! Get it? Jonathan? Firecrackers last night? Bang?"

"You are too funny," Skye said, twisting her lips into a smirk. "See you soon."

By eight o'clock, Skye had saddled Buddy, Jonathan's assigned black gelding, and she had the boy mounted, ready to start in the corral.

Along with Skye, Mr. Wheaten, Tim, and another volunteer all stood beside their assigned riders and mounts.

Skye squared her Stetson and prayed, "Lord, help me teach this kid."

Jonathan sat tall in the saddle, smiling at Skye like she was the love of his life. He wore a blue safety helmet, a brown and purple plaid shirt, blue jeans, and black leather boots with horses' heads carved in the design. "I know how to ride," he signed.

"You do?" Skye signed. "When did you learn?"

"I took lessons back home. I've been riding since I was five."

"That's great! Then this should be easy for you. Now take both reins in one hand."

"No." Jonathan shook his head sharply. "I do it this way." He took one rein in each hand and then looked beyond Skye at the waiting arena.

Skye tapped the boy's leg. Jonathan's glance shifted back to her. "No, Jonathan. That's how you ride English style. You will learn to ride Western here."

"I always ride this way!" Jonathan's hands gestured in obvious anger. Frustration swept over his face, and he yanked down the helmet, his curly hair sticking out over his bent ears. Releasing the reins, he folded his arms and put on an I-want-my-own-way pout.

Forcing a smile, Skye tied the reins into a knot and slipped them over the horn of the saddle. "There. That will make it easier for you to hold them in one hand."

"No." Jonathan shook his head, his lips pinched in defiance.

"Don't you like me anymore?"

Jonathan nodded.

"Then why don't you pay attention to what I say?"

Jonathan's hands flew into a frenzy. "I don't like when you tell me what to do!"

"Having trouble, Skye?" Mr. Wheaten said, leading his team around the corner.

"Yes," she said without turning. "He is so *stubborn*!"

"Pray for wisdom." Mr. Wheaten's voice trailed away.

"I already did!" Skye yelled back. Her attention back to the boy, she signed, "Let's try this. You hold the reins, and I'll lead Buddy around the corral. But use only one hand. Okay?"

"No!" Jonathan signed and then folded his arms tightly again.

"Then you can't ride," Skye signed. "All the horses here are trained Western. If you try English, Buddy won't work."

Jonathan flashed a look of contempt and grabbed the reins sharply from the horn. Buddy flinched, threw his head up, and took several quick steps back.

"Easy, boy!" Skye grabbed the horse's bridle and then stroked him on the neck to calm him down. She darted an angry look at Jonathan. "If you do that again, your lesson will be over!"

Sticking out his tongue, Jonathan raised his hands to his ears and wiggled his fingers. But then, as though he were the best boy in the whole world, he lit up the whole corral with a Cheshire-cat smile.

Skye set her Stetson tightly down on her forehead. "When you're ready to put those reins in one hand, then we'll walk around the corral."

Jonathan sat, arms folded, smile replaced by a pout.

Folding her arms, Skye matched Jonathan's pout with her own. She stood there a full five minutes before Jonathan gave in.

The contest of wills finally over, Jonathan grabbed the knot of the reins with one hand and promptly stuck out his tongue.

"Now we'll go around one time," Skye signed. "Then we'll turn the other way and go around again. Ease up on the reins. And don't kick him in the belly! We're just going to walk slowly. Okay?"

Jonathan's look of disgust barely allowed a skimpy nod.

Skye led the way, firmly holding Buddy's bridle as they went around the corral.

"Looks good, Skye!" Tim yelled as he walked his team on the other side of the corral. "You must be doing somethin' right!"

"I sure hope so!" Skye said. "This kid is too much."

Skye and her team completed one large circle. Stopping Buddy, she turned toward the boy. Jonathan had the look of a cardboard cowpoke, one hand on the reins, the other hand stuffed in his jeans pocket.

"Relax, Jonathan," Skye signed. "If you know how to ride, you also know the horse can sense when you're nervous."

"This is too different. I don't like it."

"It will take time, but you'll learn. I'll help you. Now we're gonna go around one more time. Ready? Here we go."

They pivoted and started in the opposite direction. As Skye led her team around the corner, Tim yelled from the other side of the corral, "Don't look now, Annie, but your rider has kicked into an English mode."

Skye stopped Buddy abruptly and spun toward the boy. Like a starched shirt, Jonathan sat with both hands on the reins and his tongue out at Skye.

"Jonathan! That's not the way I showed you!" she signed fiercely and then reached for the reins.

Before Skye knew what had happened, Jonathan yanked the reins, spinning Buddy around and knocking Skye flat on her back. The boy leaned forward in the saddle and kicked his heels sharply into Buddy's ribs. The horse let out a loud whinny, reared up, and in a flash, raced full speed ahead toward the barn.

"Jonathan!" Skye screamed as she scrambled to her feet. "Come back here!"

chapter five

Mr. Wheaten! Stop him!" Skye screamed at the top of her lungs. Leading his team around the corner, Mr. Wheaten heard Skye and looked up to see Buddy tearing across the center of the corral like a racehorse heading for his "finish line."

"Stop him, somebody!" Skye started to run after Jonathan. *If Buddy runs into the barn, Jonathan will wipe out on that door frame.*

Mr. Wheaten stood firm, not taking so much as one step forward. He grabbed a whistle hanging around his neck and blew it in two short spurts. *Tweet-tweet-tweet! Tweet-tweet-tweet!*

"What's he doing?" Skye yelled, racing after the horse.

At the sound of the whistle, Buddy's ears perked forward. Immediately, he took a sharp turn, slowed to a trot, and shuffled into a lazy walk. As though led by some phantom cowboy, the horse strolled right to the corral fence and placed his chin on the top railing. There he stood, his belly puffing and the rest of him planning to go no farther until Mr. Wheaten said so. As hard as Jonathan tried to turn him, the horse would not move.

That's right! Skye remembered. *These horses have been trained in a special way!*

She charged toward Buddy and grabbed his bridle, her desperate breaths equal to his. Her face flushed hot, and sweat oozed out all over her body, more from frazzled nerves and embarrassment than from the summer sun. Worse than that, her temper boiled like a cauldron. She was ready to rip this Jonathan kid to shreds.

You little monster! Skye fumed, staring daggers at the boy.

Jonathan relaxed back into the saddle, both hands on the reins, with a new Cheshire grin plastered all over his smug face. Already Skye knew that could mean only one thing: "I won. Ha-ha!"

"Your lesson is over!" Skye signed. There was no doubt that her hands meant business!

Picnic and field day at Camp Oneega!

Skye looked up at the clear blue canopy and filled her lungs with fresh mountain air. *A perfect day for food, fun, and games! Thank you, God,* she said silently, blocking out her disastrous morning with Jonathan. At the end of an asphalt track on a large grass field, she stood holding a black-and-white-checkered flag. Mr. Wheaten prepared to blow his whistle at the starting line to send eight wheelchair racers on their way. The excitement of the competition charged through the air like lightning.

Skye glanced at the opposite sides of the field. Two sets of bleachers hosted a cheering audience of campers and workers. Dotting the crowd were dozens of balloons, one occasionally floating away on a fickle breeze. On the field around Skye, children wearing helmets were participating in the Camp Oneega Olympics, trying their best to win a gold medal.

At one station, two teams of blind children stood in circles, handing footballs around and laughing, racing against the clock. Skye spotted Chad refereeing two other teams trying to push a gigantic inflated ball past their own goal markers at opposite ends of a grass court. *They look like ants trying to push a red gumball*, Skye mused.

At another station, she saw Morgan supervising a line of children waiting to throw beanbags through the mouth of a painted clown board. Two staff clowns were handing out candy, their antics drawing hearty laughs from all those around. Skye's attention was drawn to a spot where Linda was helping bowlers roll black plastic balls at rainbow-colored pins. Frequent cheers and bursts of applause rippled over the action, reminding Skye of football games back home at Madison High.

Late in the afternoon, the fun migrated to a picnic area next to Lake Oneega. Under a cluster of maple trees, the kitchen staff had already set up an assembly line of picnic food.

Skye helped her cabin girls go through the food line. From the cooks' side of the table where Linda was busy placing hot dogs on paper plates, Chad yelled, "Hey, Skye, could you help me out?" He promptly shoved half a hot dog into his mouth.

Skye couldn't help staring in awe at Chad's looks. His sky-blue camp shirt highlighted his blond hair, his long curly lashes lending a twinkle to his gorgeous brown eyes. Skye's heart did a funny flip, and she felt her face grow hotter than it already was from the summer sun. Then she remembered Linda.

"I'm busy!" she snapped as though her arm had absorbed a good hard pinch.

"Aw, come on, Skye," Chad begged. "Jonathan needs a chaperone, but Tim's giving paddleboat rides on the lake, and you can see Linda's busy. I need somebody who can sign, and I don't see Mrs. Wheaten anywhere. How 'bout it? The other workers will cover for you here."

Skye watched Chad intensely. His dimples deepened as he proceeded to gobble down the second half of his hot dog. Then he smiled. Despite her flipping heart, Skye's temper flared, and the sense of duty she had brought to camp floated away into the cloudless sky like a rebel balloon.

No—because of you. No—because of Linda. And no—because of Jonathan! hung on the edge of her tongue, the vicious words ready to blurt out and ruin a perfectly good day. Then, like a wisp of cool mountain air, Morgan's earlier advice brought Skye's common sense back down to earth. *Focus!* echoed in her mind. *We're here to serve the Lord!*

Get with it! Skye lectured herself. *This is business. I have a job to do.* "Oh, all right!" she finally said, her feelings buried behind a half-sincere smile. With her hands on her hips, she turned and searched for a peanut of a boy she knew brought only big-time trouble.

Skye searched in the tree shadows hosting the tables of guests. Looking for a tiny boy with a big helmet, she studied the face of every camper. Jonathan was nowhere to be found. "Chad, where is he?" she asked, a hint of panic in her voice.

"Down there under that big maple right near the gate at the dock. He's sitting on the ground with his plate on his lap. Hey, it looks like he's sharin' his supper with one of Camp Oneega' resident rodents."

Skye's glance shifted to the shade of a monstrous maple tree near the lake's edge. Sitting against the tree, Jonathan gulped down a hot dog and threw scraps to an eager squirrel.

"He's all alone," Skye whispered, and the hard truth of being deaf hit her right between the eyes.

"What was that, Skye?" Chad asked.

"Jonathan can't talk to any other campers, and they can't talk to him," Skye whispered again.

Suddenly, her heart felt a strange tug—a tug so different, yet not so different, from her heart's response to those she loved, to the Chambers family, Morgan, Chad, or even her wonderful horse. Like a cement block, a weight pushed on Skye's chest, and her heart felt like it was going to pop out her back. All at once, with no explanation, she cared. More than she thought she ever could. *God*, she prayed, *help me to love this poor little kid.*

Grabbing her food, Skye quickly made her way to the lake. Creeping toward the tree, she tried not to scare the squirrel, but it scampered away.

Jonathan looked up, displayed an unmistakable scowl, and went back to his plate. Pretending Skye wasn't even there, he busied himself by scattering scraps all over the ground. With the blue helmet resting nearby, the boy's hair had curled into tight, wet ringlets, and his cheeks were fiery red from the hot day.

Kneeling in front of him, Skye tapped Jonathan on his sneaker. He yanked his legs into a fold and focused on his plate. He gobbled down one last big chunk of hot dog smothered in ketchup, mustard, and onions.

Casually, Skye sat with her legs crossed and gently tapped Jonathan's knee.

With a pout that said loud and clear in any language, "Do not disturb," he glared at the unwelcome guest.

Skye put her plate down and gave Jonathan a warm, sincere smile. "I'm sorry for being angry with you this morning," she signed.

Jonathan took a long, deliberate drink of his soda, his dark brown eyes staring—far beyond Skye and her smile.

"Can we be friends again?" Her next breath on pause, Skye waited for Jonathan's response.

One more sip, and Jonathan focused on Skye.

"I really like you," Skye signed. "And I want to be your friend."

Jonathan sat still, not one muscle moving in his entire body. His pout said it all. But slowly his face started to betray his thoughts. He did something that few had the pleasure to see. His lips broke into a hint of a surrendering smile. "Okay. Me too," he signed, as though there had never been a debate about it. Grabbing his plate, he took great care picking up every tiny crumb, all of which found their way to his mouth. Again, he looked at Skye and, this time, gave her the benefit of his finest grin.

Skye returned a smile then looked back for Chad. At the rows of tables, the rest of the campers were having the time of their lives. Enjoying one another, the food, and the perfect weather, they unintentionally displayed no concern for Jonathan Martin.

Life goes on without the deaf boy, Skye thought.

For the next half hour, Skye and Jonathan talked about their favorite things. At the top of the list were horses, motorcycles, and the best computer games ever.

"Hey, Skye!" Mr. Wheaten's voice boomed from the tables. "The picnic's over! We'll help get your kids back to the cabin for cleanup and then their art class. Would you please stay with Jonathan until Tim's finished on the lake? He'll be done in fifteen minutes."

"Sure thing, Mr. Wheaten!" Skye yelled back. "I'll take Jonathan for a walk along the lake and wait for Tim to come ashore."

Skye stood and watched the other campers start to snail-trail their way from the picnic tables, across the field, and to their cabins. Jonathan stood, tucked his helmet under his arm, and started to walk away.

Skye touched his shoulder. "No, you stay with me," she signed. "We're gonna walk around the lake and wait for Tim. Okay?"

"Okay!" Jonathan's radiant smile lit up his whole face.

Skye picked up Jonathan's plate, threw all the paper products into a can, and she and Jonathan headed off on a walkway that encircled the entire lake.

"Hey, Tim!" Skye called to her co-worker out on a paddleboat with a camper. "How's the water?"

"Cool! Real cool!" Tim yelled back. "I'd rather be in it than on it! Who've ya got there with you?"

"Your friend and mine! He'll be waitin' when you come ashore!"

"Okay, Skye, see you in a few minutes!" Tim turned the paddleboat in another direction.

Skye felt a gentle poke on her arm. Jonathan had her attention.

"Can I ride that?" he signed. "That looks like fun."

"It's too late now," Skye signed. "Maybe tomorrow."

Jonathan lowered his head and kicked at the ground, sending a puff of dirt and loose stones into the lake.

Skye touched him on his arm, her face bubbling with a new thought. "I know what we can do! Let's collect leaves, and later we can make a scrapbook."

Jonathan's eyes brightened, his radiant smile returning. "Okay," he signed. "Where do we start?"

"Just look around. There are all kinds of trees along this path."

All around the lake, Skye pointed to an array of interesting trees. She named a maple, birch, scrub pine, beech, oak, elm, and several others she knew. She showed Jonathan how to carefully pinch off leaves from low-hanging branches. In a few excited, scrambling minutes, he had a small collection, ready to start his own scrapbook.

"Let's rest a minute," Skye told Jonathan. She looked across the pond where Tim was parking the paddleboat at the dock. She turned back to Jonathan, ready to sign—

But Jonathan was gone!

"Where is he now?" Skye let out a frustrated sigh, then a spark of panic widened her eyes. *Water—deep water—and woods—lots of woods!* Frantic thoughts flooded her mind. *He could be anywhere! In seconds!*

Cupping her hands over her eyes, Skye strained, searching the edge of the lake, reaching into the shadows of the nearby woods. She heard movement—off to the side, on a darkened path. She ran toward the sound, deeper into the woods that led her right to where she hoped Jonathan had gone. A few feet in front of her, the elusive boy stood, swinging a stick as long as his body at something up in a tree.

"Jonathan, what are you doing?" Skye yelled, running toward him. Brown eyes flashing, Skye now saw what the boy was about to whack.

Ahead on a sturdy oak branch hung a strange, gray object. Bigger than a football, it resembled a gigantic papier-mâché Christmas ornament. Skye knew this was trouble, big trouble, and terror filled her heart.

Running toward Jonathan, she tried desperately to grab the stick from his swinging arms. "Jonathan! No!" she screamed, knowing he couldn't hear. "Hornets!"

chapter six

The next morning, Skye and Jonathan showed up at breakfast with the "White Blotch Plague." Polka dots of itch ointment covered their bodies, and Skye's upper lip was swollen. Jonathan sat fidgeting and signing with Tim at their cabin's table. Skye was busy answering a zillion questions about all her spots while she helped the Five Ferns kids get their food and sit down. Her attitude was anything but cheerful. Frankly, she was tired of all the pointing, giggles, and stupid jokes.

"Have you seen Mr. Wheaten?" she asked Morgan. "I'm so frustrated with Jonathan—I've gotta talk to the boss."

Morgan wheeled to her place at the Five Ferns table. "Nope, haven't seen him yet. Oh—there he is—coming in now." She pointed toward the door.

Starting toward Mr. Wheaten, Skye yelled back to Morgan, "Looks like all our kids have their act together. I'll be right back."

"Okay. We're cool."

Skye weaved her way around several tables busy with clanging dishes and noisy chatter. Just as Mr. Wheaten made his way to the breakfast line, Skye joined him.

"Sir, could I please speak to you sometime today?" she asked.

"Well, if it isn't Annie Oakley with white freckles!" Mr. Wheaten let loose a hearty laugh. "I heard about your buzzin' adventure down at the lake yesterday. What can I do for you, little lady?"

Buzzin' adventure — yeah, right! Skye flipped her pigtails back and scratched a white spot on her arm. "It's good that Jonathan and I aren't allergic to hornet stings. All we're doing now is fighting off the itches. I really need to see you, if that's okay."

"Why, sure, little lady." Mr. Wheaten pulled a small notebook out of his shirt pocket. "Let's see. I've got a free half hour right after breakfast." He glanced at his watch. "How about eight o'clock, or are you busy with an activity?"

"Nope, I'm free then."

"Well, then, you just mosey on over to my office, and we'll have a little chat." Mr. Wheaten's belly pushed his tray along the food line with hardly any help from his hands.

"Thanks, Mr. Wheaten. I'll be there."

At eight o'clock sharp, Skye showed up at Mr. Wheaten's office in the registration building.

"Come in, Annie!" Sitting behind the desk, Mr. Wheaten tipped his black Stetson at Skye. "And have yourself a seat."

Skye relaxed into a canvas lawn chair in front of a huge desk that looked like the outside of a log cabin. The room, paneled with barn boards, displayed plastic models of horses and steers on every flat surface. A file cabinet in one corner held a wooden lamp carved like a prancing horse. A pair of gigantic steer horns filled the wall space behind the desk. Underneath the horns was displayed a handsome framed document, which read:

TEXAS LONGHORNS
QUARTERBACK
JUNIOR/SENIOR YEARS

Mr. Wheaten's desk looks like a disaster ready to happen, Skye thought. Files and papers littered the surface along with a phone, a baseball glove and ball, a cluster of empty Dr. Pepper soda cans, a stack of books with a Bible on top, and a shiny metal Texas longhorn paperweight. Skye found herself giggling at the chaotic display.

"What's ticklin' your funny bone, little lady?" Mr. Wheaten laughed, took off his hat, and tossed it up over his right shoulder. As though it knew right where to go, the hat landed perfectly on one of the horn tips. "It wouldn't be any of my housekeepin' skills now, would it?"

"I wish my mother could see this office," Skye said, giggling. "Just give her about ten minutes, and she'd have this place looking like something in a home decorating magazine."

Mr. Wheaten leaned back in his chair and placed his hands behind his head. "Well, little lady, this room's ready now for a magazine: *Bad Housekeepin'*!" He let loose another hearty chuckle, and then his face grew serious. "Now, what would you like to discuss with me?"

"Mr. Wheaten, I don't know how to help Jonathan. He's drivin' me nuts," Skye complained, flipping back her pigtails. "He says he likes me, but as soon as my back is turned, he does something stupid that gets him in trouble. He could get hurt—or he could hurt someone else—or Buddy!"

The man folded his arms and relaxed into his chair. "Annie, I told you when you first came that he'd be a handful. Let me clue you in on a little secret. Jonathan is a very lonely hombre. There are no other deaf kids anywhere near where he lives. He has no brothers or sisters, and his father—well—let's just say, his father has no time for his son. I think Mrs. Martin tries to make up for all that by giving Jonathan his own way. Even Christians have their problems."

"Why did they send him here for the whole summer?"

"Well, it was mostly Mrs. Martin's decision. Mr. Martin doesn't seem to care one way or another what Jonathan does. But Jonathan's mother was hoping that her son would get to know other deaf kids—or even hearing kids. From watching them, he would learn how to behave. She knows we have Bible classes and chapel services, two ways we can teach him the right way to act. It's too bad there aren't any other hearing-impaired campers here right now. But we're expecting a few more in the next couple of weeks. That should help."

Skye stared at the desk clutter, recalling the two disasters she had suffered with Jonathan already. "I don't know what I can do to make him listen. He's—he's—impossible!"

"Nothing's impossible with God, Annie. You have to be a little patient. Nonetheless, I can split your time with Tim and Linda if you want—"

"No—no—it's not that! I want to help him! I studied sign language all winter long to help him. I just don't know how!"

"All good things take time, Annie. You two haven't even been here a full week. We have to remember that God performs his work in his own good time. Miracles do happen—and at Camp Oneega I've seen many a miracle. Just let Christ's love show through you, and don't give up too soon. You may well be part of a miracle in this young man's life."

"Okay. I'll keep praying and smiling—and signing. Maybe one of these times, Jonathan and I will connect. I don't want anyone to get hurt, that's all."

"Love never fails, Annie." Mr. Wheaten leaned forward on his desk. "Anything else, little lady?"

"Could we pray about this? Now?" Skye asked. " I—"

R-r-r-ring!

Mr. Wheaten picked up the phone. "Bossman here!" he bellowed. "What can I do for you?"

Skye studied the man's face, a deep concern sweeping over it like a flooding tide. "He did what? I'll be right there," Mr. Wheaten said. All in one quick motion, the man slammed the phone down and grabbed his hat. "C'mon, Skye. Looks like we've got big trouble—again!"

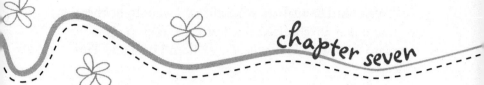
kye and Mr. Wheaten hurried out of the office and headed toward the center of camp. Crossing the road, they hustled around the left side of the barn. Skye looked beyond a cluster of trees and small playground to the Olympic-size pool. The water, silent and smooth, glistened from the sun creeping up in a haze of summer blue. Hints of chlorine scented the air, its brazen odor teasing Skye's nose.

"What did he do now?" Skye blurted out in frustration. "It's only eight fifteen in the morning! Isn't he supposed to be in a Bible class?"

"Linda just called me from the pool," Mr. Wheaten said. "Somehow, Jonathan got it into his head that he wanted to go swimming—now."

"Now?"

"Yes, now. And, somehow, he got out of his class without being seen. Linda was busy cleaning the pool and spotted him. When she tried to stop him from jumping in—with his clothes on!—he pushed her in."

Good riddance! "Is she okay?" Skye forced out.

"Yeah, she's all right—just embarrassed. And when Tim got there, Jonathan had locked himself in the girls' locker room."

"Wait until he realizes where he is! I want to be there for that one!" Skye huffed at a fast pace to keep up with the man. "But why do you need me? Both Linda and Tim can sign."

"Well, Tim should be on his way back to the class where his cabin kids are. You've spent more time with Jonathan than Linda has. If anyone can get through to him, it'll be you."

Linda stood waiting at the open gate of the chain-link fence that surrounded the pool. Her blond hair hung in long wet strands over her shoulders. Soaked from the surprise dunking, her terrycloth robe clung to her like wet paper. Her face was drenched with embarrassment. "He's still in there!" She pointed to the locker room.

"You have a key for that, don't you?" Mr. Wheaten rushed through the gate. Skye followed.

"Well, yeah," Linda said, "but I was afraid he might club me with something."

Oh, super chicken on top of everything else! Skye stared at her fiercely.

"Skye, I want you to go in for him." Mr. Wheaten pulled a set of keys from his belt loop. He hurried to the locker room and stuck a key in the door.

"What if he won't come out?" Skye asked, doubting the confidence Mr. Wheaten had placed in her.

"Just be patient," Mr. Wheaten said, "and love him. He has to know that we do care for him in spite of his bad behavior."

"Yeah," Linda said, "and tell him I'm not mad at him for pushing me into the pool."

Mr. Wheaten pulled open the heavy door. "Skye, I'll give you five minutes. If he won't come out, tell him I'm comin' in."

46

"Yeah." Linda glanced at her watch. "Soon this place will be crawling with girls. We start lessons at eight thirty."

Skye stepped inside, the powerful smell of disinfectant greeting her from the room's early morning scrub. She studied every corner and bench in the large, hollow room. Not one trace of Jonathan—

Skerwoo-o-o-sh! From the bathroom at the far end, a loud flush broke the silence.

Maybe the poor kid's sick, Skye thought and ran toward the noise.

Straight ahead in the adjoining room, a toilet flushed again from one of four special-needs stalls lining the back wall. However, no skinny legs stood in any of them.

Skerwoo-o-o-sh!

Okay, kid, where are you? Skye hurried toward the line of stalls, pulling open each door until she came to the third one. Locked!

She knelt down and then peeked under the stainless-steel partition. Inside, Jonathan sat against the wall on the back of the toilet, knees bent, and feet propped on the seat.

Skerwoo-o-o-sh! With his elbow poking the button on the wall, he sent a bowl of water on its merry way. The boy's eyes flashed at Skye, and his lips gave way to a nasty tongue followed by his same old mischievous grin.

Pulling out from under the partition, Skye maneuvered onto her back, and, again, slid under the wall. Flat on the floor, she raised her hands to sign. She peered at the boy with a smile as fake as her love for Linda. "What are you doing in here?" Her angry eyes said it long before her hands did.

"I'm watching the water go around. It's fun."

"Jonathan!" she signed with an exclamation point. "You should be in Bible class. Let's go!"

"No! I wanna go swimming."

"Your cabin goes swimming at two o'clock. You need to leave."

"No!"

Kaboom! Skye's anger exploded and her face turned red hot. *If I get my hands on you, you little*—she fumed. Then she remembered why she was there, why she had volunteered her whole summer to work at Camp Oneega. To help kids. To help difficult kids. Just like she used to be. *Yeah, I know, Lord. This kid needs help just like I did. Help me to help him.*

Skye wiggled forward a few inches and then bent her legs completely into the stall. Propping herself against the door, she folded her arms, her brain calculating the next strategy in the latest Nicholson-Martin battle of the wills.

Skerwoo-o-o-sh! Jonathan poked the button, sending more water down the tubes. He folded his arms and smiled, his face exuberant with "I'm winning!"

"Poke the button once for me, Jonathan, okay?" Skye signed. A stingy smile betrayed her intense frustration and then—"I know what'll work!" she said to herself.

"Jonathan, you still have all your leaves, don't you?" she signed.

"Yeah. They're back at my cabin."

Skerwoo-o-o-sh!

"Well, why do you want to sit in here on such a great day? The sun's bright, you've got things to do, and after your swimming time, we can make that leaf scrapbook together. It's no fun being in here by yourself, is it? Hey, this is the girls' bathroom. Do you want to be in here when the girls come in?"

"What?" A look of horror swept over Jonathan as his eyes bulged and his ears turned bright red. Jumping up, his skinny legs straddled the toilet. "Girls' bathroom? Get me outta here!" he signed and then reached over Skye's body, threw open the latch, and charged out of the stall.

Skye scrambled to her feet and stopped the door from swinging shut. Jonathan tore through the locker room and ran outside like every girl in camp was after him. Skye started to giggle, but in seconds, her delight turned into one sidesplitting laugh. "Thanks, God," she said. "I guess I said the magic word—'girls.' I don't think Jonathan will ever pull this stunt again."

chapter eight

I t was the end of the first week, and Saturday morning arrived at Camp Oneega with a rush of cool mountain air and bright sunshine. A perfect day for a trail ride!

Inside the corral, Skye wiped down her horse using a cloth drenched with bug repellent. Next to Champ, ten more horses stood at the fence, saddled and ready to go. Mr. Wheaten and Chad were busy making last-minute checks of all the gear and horses' hooves.

"Chad, I'm glad you could go along since Tim's baling hay today," Mr. Wheaten said and then yelled to Skye, "And little lady, looks like you're ready to go with that fancy western outfit on. You look more like Annie Oakley than she did!"

"Thanks!" Skye giggled and then glanced over her shoulder to the outside of the corral, where eight campers wearing helmets and jackets waited with their chaperones. "And it looks like they're all ready too."

Five children, all standing, squirmed as though they had ants marching up their legs. The others fidgeted in their wheelchairs. Several in the lineup blended loud grunts with laughter while their arms beat the air, their only way of expressing delight for this very special day. In the middle of the line stood one camper Skye knew only too well. *I can't believe Jonathan is going.*

"Okay, Chad," Mr. Wheaten said, glancing at his watch, "let's get the kids mounted. I wanna hit the trail no later than nine o'clock. Skye, will you give the horses one last wipe-down with bug juice? And give yourself one, as well. This cool air helps, but I'm sure we'll run into an army of nasty flies on our way. Get the horses' ears and bellies real good."

"Will do." Skye's glance followed Mr. Wheaten and Chad as they walked toward the gate. Despite a promise she had made to herself earlier, she stared holes through Chad.

Peering out from the shade of a dark brown Stetson, his brown eyes practically knocked her off her feet. *Whoa!* Skye's heart thumped so loud she was sure Chad would hear it. *No big deal. It's only Chad—Linda's Chad. Knock it off.* But her heart thumped as though she had just done the trail ride, out and back, without a horse! Quickly her attention shifted to the task, and she trailed after Mr. Wheaten and Chad.

"Sir, one quick question," Skye said.

He stopped and faced Skye. "What is it, Annie?"

"I see that Jonathan's going with us. Are you sure that's a good idea after—after all the trouble he's caused this past week? I mean, he's not exactly in the running for the 'Camper of the Week' trophy."

"I put a lot of prayer into this one, little lady." Mr. Wheaten shot a quick glance at Jonathan. "I decided to allow him to go for two reasons. One: I saw your last report stating that he finished the week's riding lessons on pretty good terms with you and Buddy. Two: I think Jonathan needs to know that we don't hold grudges. He already did lose a few privileges. I don't want to take everything from him, or it'll be an awfully long summer—for all of us."

"So we're gonna pray him up and down the mountain?" Skye's voice displayed obvious disbelief.

Mr. Wheaten let loose a belly-bouncing laugh as he joined Chad outside the corral. "I guess you could put it that way. Besides, the horses are practically nose to tail all the way up to the secret campsite and back. What could the rascal do when he'll be almost hog-tied in the middle of a horse parade?"

"What could he do?" Skye said. "Jonathan's, like, the Master of Disaster. If there's a way to cause a crisis, he'll find it."

"Skye, I sure hope you're wrong," Chad yelled over the railing.

Well, I certainly was wrong about you! Skye wanted to say as she retreated to horse debugging one more time.

In minutes, Chad and Mr. Wheaten had all the campers mounted on special high-back saddles, legs secured with Velcro straps. After Mr. Wheaten prayed, the trail ride began, eleven horses in a straight line.

The trail boss led the horse train out of the corral with Skye in the middle, directly in front of Jonathan so he could see her sign. Chad brought up the rear. The horses clip-clopped on the tarred road around the barn. They passed the pool already filled with campers splashing, screaming, and having a wonderful time.

"Hey, Linda!" Chad yelled to the blonde lifeguard.

"What's happening, Chad honey?" she yelled back.

Sickening! Skye fumed.

Crossing at an intersection, the horses made their way down along the waterslide to the trail that snaked its way behind Lake Oneega and into a forest.

For the next hour, they ambled on a beaten path through alternating woods and open fields in the Shamokin State Park that joined Camp Oneega. The trail, wide enough for a four-wheeler, led them along a trickling brook through sweet-smelling pines.

Gently up the mountainside the trail weaved, leveling off into a forest as thick as bristles on a giant paintbrush. Every twenty minutes, Mr. Wheaten stopped, giving the horses a chance to sip from the gushing stream. He, Skye, and Chad checked saddle cinches, Velcro, and bridle straps.

"Last stop before reaching camp!" Mr. Wheaten yelled, mounting his horse one more time. "We'll be there in about fifteen minutes! Let's move 'em out!"

Skye signed to Jonathan and then glanced ahead. Like a brown ribbon, the trail crossed a wooden bridge a few dozen yards ahead and then lost itself in towering pines as it disappeared around a giant bluff. "Good boy, Champ," Skye said, petting her horse's neck. "You're probably soakin' this up as much as I am."

Deeper into the ravine they went, and Skye found it impossible to sit still on Champ's back. The beauty of God's creation swept over her as though it were a flood of water itself. In every direction, the woods and its wonders greeted her.

Gentle breezes tickled the trees, quivering their branches and setting their leaves into a dance of joy. Moss-covered jagged rocks on each side of the trail oozed trickles of water, as though their assigned duty was to announce the next spectacular display, Oneega Falls.

Skye took a deep breath, and the smell of "green" filled every part of her being. Her gaze darted to one side of the upcoming bridge, at water's edge, where about a half-dozen tiny blue butterflies fluttered to the babbles of the rushing brook. The thunderous falls now overpowered the air, blocking out all other sounds.

"Keep the horses close to one another over the bridge!" Mr. Wheaten yelled. "They'll do better staring at a tail right in front of them than watching the water on both sides!"

"Keep Buddy close to Champ when we cross the bridge," Skye signed to Jonathan.

"Listen, kids! Oneega Falls!" Mr. Wheaten yelled at the top of his lungs as the horses clip-clopped across the thick wooden planks. "Our secret campsite is just beyond that!"

"Oneega Falls is just ahead," Skye signed to Jonathan. *Too bad he can't hear that amazing sound.*

Across the bridge, the horses made their way around one last bluff. The trail widened into a flat area that led to a shoreline of stones and gravel. Straight ahead Oneega Falls roared, a majestic display of God's beauty and power.

Lining up their horses, the riders sat gawking at nature's water show half a football field away. Far above their heads, the falls flooded over a table of flat rocks arrayed on both sides by the greenest trees Skye had ever seen.

The water thundered as it crashed down over more layers of rocks, tumbling, tumbling, until it splashed onto large boulders level with the riders. There, billows of white foam faded into ripples that quickly smoothed into a serene pool as clear as glass.

A rainbow arched in a stream of sunlight. Off to one side the pool overflowed, forming the gushing stream that had found its way down the mountain to form Oneega Lake. Fed by the falls, a steady breeze and fine mist saturated the cool air around the riders, welcoming them to the secret and special place.

"Wow, God, you outdid yourself this time!" Skye said, her eyes feasting on the beauty before her.

From the campers, a chorus of hearty giggles and grunts joined Skye's approval. Arms waved and hands clapped in a concert of praise.

Glancing back at Jonathan, Skye found it easy to smile. The boy's blue helmet, already glossed over with mist, framed his beaming face, eyes wide with awe.

Skye waved to catch the boy's attention. "Isn't that cool?"

"Yes!" Jonathan smiled.

"God made that," Skye signed.

"I know," he signed.

"Okay, gang," Mr. Wheaten yelled, pointing. "Follow me. The campsite is over there, just beyond reach of this mist!"

Skye tugged Champ's reins to the right. Leaning forward, she stood in her stirrups and stretched to see beyond the riders in front. Straight ahead, she eyed a small clearing a stone's throw away. Amid a cluster of trees, the hidden campsite nestled against another large bluff.

In the center a small campfire already glowed, and a table displayed food supplies and a beverage cooler. Three cooks, including Morgan, with chef's hats, spatulas, and smiles waited around the fire. Behind them, a wall of bushes half concealed a camp pickup truck.

For the next three hours, the trail riders "hid away." Hungry mouths devoured ham, home fries, and beans, Mr. Wheaten's favorite, as soon as the food was cooked on the open flames. Next, Chad pulled his guitar from the truck, and the campers sat around the fire singing, clapping, and laughing.

I'm in some kind of music warp! Skye mused, as every chorus she had ever known was sung at least four times. "I'm in the Lord's Army" got five encores, the campers marching in place or saluting Mr. Wheaten until their tired bodies could hardly move. Skye's arms felt like lead weights from signing every last song with Jonathan, who was always ready to do just one more.

Chad, with a string of "the dumbest jokes in the world" and dumber songs, had the campers practically rolling on their sides while Skye and Mr. Wheaten helped the kitchen staff clean up. As busy as she was, Skye found it impossible not to focus on Chad, his antics forcing her smirks into frenzies of giggles.

One o'clock and time to head back! Mr. Wheaten secured the last camper on a horse while Skye and Chad went down the line, checking straps and cinches. Then as Skye mounted Champ, Chad came walking past.

"Annie, do you want me to check your cinch too?" Chad joked. From the Stetson's shadow, his brown eyes sparkled all the way to his dimples, sending Skye's heart halfway up her throat.

Whoa! Skye's face turned red hot despite the mountain chill. *I sure would! Oh, but then there's Linda!* "No thank you! I'm fine!" she snapped without even a hint of a smile.

"What? Oh, okay." Chad squared his hat and started to walk away. "Later."

"Let's move 'em out!" Mr. Wheaten yelled.

The campers took one last look and then waved at the water as the horses started out.

"Goodbye, falls!" Skye yelled and waved. "We had fun!"

Over the gravel flat the horses walked, then weaved their way around the bluff to the one-hour trail that led them back down the ravine.

Skye spotted the bridge ahead with the stream bubbling beneath. Pivoting in her saddle, she signed to Jonathan, "Remember to keep Buddy close behind Champ now. We don't need any horses straying out of line when we cross that narrow bridge."

"Okay." Jonathan gave a convincing smile.

As Mr. Wheaten's horse started across the bridge, Skye turned to sign just in time to see Jonathan, grin still set, yanking Buddy's reins to the right. The horse's head flew in the air, and then he pivoted abruptly. Jonathan kicked his mount in the ribs and slapped the reins across its neck. In a chain reaction, each horse behind him, not sure what to do next, balked, and then stepped out of line or turned in frantic circles.

"Skye, stop Jonathan!" Chad yelled. "He's scaring all the horses!"

Halfway across the bridge, Mr. Wheaten turned and yelled, "Don't anybody move. I've got my whistle!"

But it was too late. In seconds, Buddy had bounded out of line and was charging down the embankment with Jonathan prodding him right into the cascading stream.

"Jonathan!" Skye screamed. "What are you doing?"

plash! Before Mr. Wheaten could tweet, Buddy had barreled down the steep bank in a half-run, half-slide. He slipped on some rocks and tumbled into the stream headfirst. When the horse tripped, his front legs collapsed, and Jonathan went flying out of the saddle like a human cannonball. He landed on the other side of the stream, his top half on the muddy embankment, the rest in the water. He lay motionless while Buddy regained his footing, sloshed out of the water, and stumbled up the slope. The horse stood dripping wet and quivering, his front right knee a mass of blood.

"Chad," Mr. Wheaten yelled, jumping off his horse and running down the embankment, "get the kids and their horses calmed down! Skye, the first-aid kit's in my saddlebags. Bring it to me!"

Skye flew off Champ's back, retrieved the kit, and rushed down to the streambed where Mr. Wheaten was already helping Jonathan stand. The boy's cockeyed helmet, along with the top half of his skinny frame, was covered with mud and grit. The rest of him was soaked to the bone.

Mr. Wheaten gently turned Jonathan to look him square in the eyes. "Thank the Lord he had his helmet on," the man said to Skye. "Ask him if anything hurts."

Skye set the kit down and signed.

"This," Jonathan said, holding his right arm up.

Carefully, Mr. Wheaten probed the boy.

"Does that hurt?" Skye asked every time Mr. Wheaten touched him.

"No." Jonathan shook his head.

"Ah, here's the problem," Mr. Wheaten said, seeing a bloody elbow. "It's all scraped open. Looks like a little bit of a cut there too. We need to get antiseptic on that. Skye, tell him he should go all the way into the stream and clean off that mud. Then we'll fix his arm."

"Is he okay?" Chad yelled from the lineup on the bridge.

"Yeah," Mr. Wheaten said, glancing at Buddy. "Just a couple of scratches. Looks like that's all that's wrong with the horse too."

"Should I check Buddy?" Skye asked.

"No, I'll do it." Mr. Wheaten started walking up the slope. "You tell Jonathan what I want him to do, and open the kit. Get the antiseptic — and some bandages. I guess you were right, Annie," Mr. Wheaten added. "He *is* the Master of Disaster."

Skye touched Jonathan, who was already busy adjusting his helmet, and she took a deep breath. *I have just about had it with you*, she had right on the tips of her fingers. Smiling at this moment was the farthest thing from her mind. "Jonathan, what were you doing?" Her hands chopped angrily at the air.

"I like water!" he signed. Then that same sly grin, even through the mud on his face, proclaimed another Martin victory. "And I wanted to see if Buddy liked water too!"

Skye's second week at Camp Oneega found her homesick for Mom and Dad Chambers, fuming at Chad, and totally frustrated with Jonathan.

Hot, humid weather had settled on the camp like a wet blanket. Because of the muggy heat, all horse-related activities had either been moved to early morning or were cancelled. More Bible classes, arts and crafts, and chapel services helped fill the void each day, along with unlimited swim time and water games at the slide and lake. After lunch on Wednesday, everyone welcomed the chapel service in the air-conditioned gym.

Onstage, Skye sat with nine others in the staff "orchestra," playing her violin while the campers sang choruses. Next to her sat guitar-strumming Chad, whom she tried to totally ignore. Mr. Wheaten, dressed like a clown, played a recorder and encouraged the kids to sing their hearts out as he led the music. For the next part of the program a girls' trio sang "Jesus Loves Me."

Mr. Wheaten answered his cell phone and then leaned toward Skye. "Annie, we need you to sign the rest of the service to Jonathan," he whispered. "My wife just called. She has a migraine."

"What about Tim and Linda?"

"Tim went with Bill for supplies, and—well—I've seen Linda sign. You'll handle this much better."

"Oh, great! I can't do this! I've never signed a service before." Skye's voice conveyed raw panic.

"C'mon. You'll do fine. Just go down there and sit on that chair in front of Jonathan. All you have to do is sign what's happenin' up here. It's a piece of cake. You can do it."

"Mr. Wheaten, I can't."

"Sure you can. You have to. There's nobody else. Now go on."

Skye swallowed the golf ball in her throat, and her heart raced like she had run ten miles. *Me? Sign? In front of all these kids* and *the staff?* She gulped again—hard—then placed her violin on the chair. Slowly she made her way down off the stage like she was marching to the firing squad. *I can't do this!* she told herself. *The whole world is watching.*

She sat on the folding chair in front of Jonathan, the sole occupant of the front pew. *I know just how you feel, kid,* she thought, *totally alone.* Her mind went blank. She stared at the pew, wanting to crawl under it. Not one sign she had learned made its way through the fuzz cluttering her brain. *Dear God, I need you. Help!* Skye prayed as she stared at Jonathan. Softly a hand touched her shoulder, and she looked back into Mr. Wheaten's painted clown face.

"Just sign from your heart, little lady," he said, smiling. "Do it for the Lord."

"Okay, I'll try," she said with more assurance than she felt.

"That's all we ask," he said, hustling back up on the stage. "Now, boys and girls," he boomed through the microphone, "we're gonna praise the Lord by doing three skits and singing a big bunch of songs."

The room erupted in applause, laughs, and scattered grunts.

Skits. Oh, great! Skye grimaced. *I don't know how to do skits!*

Sign from your heart, Mr. Wheaten's words echoed, so she began.

Onstage, Chad and three other volunteers performed a skit about the Good Samaritan and being nice to your neighbor. "But who is your neighbor?" Chad directed his scripted words to the girl next to him.

"The Bible says that your neighbor is anyone who needs help," she answered.

Embarrassed by her inability, Skye's face flushed hot while she struggled to make sense with her signs. Jonathan's eyes darted back and forth, to the skit, back to Skye. The actors might as well have been speaking Russian. Skye had to sign many strange words like "Samaritan," "traveler," "Pharisee." She had to spell them—slowly. Soon she trailed four or five sentences behind. Jonathan let out a string of yawns, his eyes heavy with sleep. Before long he slumped down, rested his head on the back of the pew, and closed his eyes.

"Duh!" Skye mumbled to herself. "Something tells me I'm not getting through—at all!" Reaching out her foot, she kicked Jonathan's sneaker, jolting him awake.

"Who is your n-e-i-g-h-b-o-r?" Skye signed.

"Mr. Wilson," Jonathan signed back with sleepy hands. "He lives across the street and has two dogs."

"That's not what I meant," Skye signed angrily. "It's a question from the skit!"

Shrugging his shoulders, Jonathan threw his hands up in despair. "I don't understand."

"Oh, never mind," Skye signed.

Unfortunately, the next two skits were no easier.

"Has Jesus made your heart clean?" Skye signed.

"I didn't know my heart was dirty," Jonathan answered, his eyes barely open.

"Did Jesus ever come into your heart?"

"Nope. He won't fit," Jonathan signed. Finally, he stretched out on the pew and fell fast asleep.

Skye's hands fell silent on her lap. Frustrated beyond words, spoken or signed, she sat staring at the child who had won again. Or had he? *There's so much he doesn't understand*, she reasoned, *especially about Jesus.* Fighting back tears and that golf-ball feeling in her throat, Skye's face grew hotter. As Mr. Wheaten began the choruses, Jonathan lay as still as a newborn baby, sound asleep, oblivious of the fun all around him.

Hot liquid streamed down Skye's cheeks, but brushing the tears away only made room for more. "I can't help you. I don't know how," she cried. Out the side door she ran until she reached a cluster of trees. Slumping to the ground, she buried her face in her arms and sobbed.

"Skye, what's the matter?" a familiar voice sounded concerned. "I saw you running out. Are you okay?" A hand softly touched her shoulder.

It was Chad. *Linda's Chad!*

"Oh, just leave me alone!" Skye snapped without looking up.

"You're not sick, are you?"

"No, I'm not sick," she wailed. "I'm fine. Just leave me alone."

"Then what the heck's wrong? You've been actin' funny since we got here."

"Well, if you don't know, I'm not gonna tell you," Skye growled. Then looking up into his brown eyes, her tone softened. "Please—Chad—just leave me alone."

Chad's genuine concern curbed his dimpled smile. "Okay, if that's what you want. But I'm here anytime you need me. Just ask." Turning away, he walked back through the door.

Inside, the campers sang at the top of their lungs while the building swayed to "I'm in the Lord's Army."

And outside all alone, Skye cried as though she had lost one of the best friends she ever had. Maybe she had.

edtime and lights-out in all the cabins. While the Five Ferns girls slept soundly, Skye and Morgan sat in their cabin's bathroom with the door shut tight. Skye was crying her eyes out again while Morgan held a box of tissues and fed her a steady supply.

"I wanna go home!" Skye tried to muffle her wail. She blew her nose for the umpteenth time and banked the soggy tissue ball off the wall into the waste can. "I can't help that kid. He's ruining my life!"

Morgan sat still and relaxed. The day's activities had taken their toll on her body, so much that her freckles even seemed pale. "Skye, cool it!" she whispered. "You keep forgetting one little thing."

"What?"

"You can't cure all these kids' problems by yourself. In fact, you can't cure them at all. This is teamwork—you, me, the staff, and God. He's got to do the fixing. We're just here to show his love. You will get through to Jonathan, but it'll take time. For Pete's sake, we've only been here a little over a week, and the whole summer is ahead of us. So just take a deep breath!"

"But he won't listen—to me—to anyone."

"And who does that remind you of? Huh? Somebody very near and dear to both of us. You! And not too long ago at that."

"Oh, Morgan, stop always reminding me of my past."

"Hey, Skye, my past's nothing to be proud of either, but God gave both of us one more chance with Mr. and Mrs. Chambers. I don't think we should forget that. And we can't stop praying for these kids. Ever."

Skye filled another tissue and bounced it into the can. "Oh, I guess you're right. You're always right when it comes to these things. But what am I gonna do about Chad?"

"Chad, schmad." Morgan frowned in disgust. "Remember—and I've said this before—he's not yours. You've never even dated. You know Mr. and Mrs. C.'s rules about that."

"Date? Yeah, right. I won't see that day until I'm sixteen. By then he'll probably be in college or married or something."

"You know, you're ridiculous. What if—what if—what if! How many times have Mr. and Mrs. C. and Pastor Newman told us to not worry and to trust in God? The right one will come along."

"But it hurts so bad when I see him with Linda," Skye cried.

"You're telling me?" Morgan flipped back her red curls. "Remember last year how I had it so bad for Drew? He didn't even know I existed. But I'm over him now."

"Yeah, and what's this with you and Caleb?" Skye forced a smile after hours of nothing but tears.

"Caleb? He is such a doll." Morgan couldn't help but giggle. "And Drew is history. Skye, that's the way it'll be with you and Chad. It'll either happen or it won't. Just give it to the Lord."

Suddenly, Skye's entire body felt limp. Her throat burned, and her eyelids felt like lead weights. Through the tears, she strained to see her watch. "Wow! It's almost midnight," she whispered.

"Yeah," Morgan said as she reached back and opened the door. "We'll both feel and look like dog meat tomorrow if we don't hit the sack now."

"Morgan," Skye said softly.

"Yeah?"

"Thanks. Thanks a lot."

"No problem, sis."

"Let's pray for Jonathan right now," Skye said.

"And for us," Morgan added. "We need all the prayer we can get."

The next day brought cooler weather, so Skye had another riding lesson with Jonathan. In one of those rare times, the lesson went fine with Jonathan behaving and Skye controlling her temper. The rest of Skye's morning activities passed with no crises. By lunchtime, she felt like her life was back on track, not only with Jonathan but also with her feelings about Chad.

In the cafeteria, Skye and Morgan helped their cabin girls get lunch trays and settle down. Skye sat at the Five Ferns table and watched Tim and his cabin boys line up with their trays for food. She spotted Jonathan halfway back in the line and burst out laughing.

"Morgan," Skye yelled to the other end of the table, "look at Jonathan. He looks too ridiculous for words. Sometimes he can be as cute as a puppy."

Morgan turned and burst out laughing too. "He looks like some weird insect from another planet," she yelled back to Skye. "Too cool."

Jonathan had made his appearance in the food line wearing a gigantic pair of sunglasses with red and white frames striped like a candy cane. Poking the glasses back on his nose to keep them in place, he had quite a time sliding his tray along. The arms of the glasses wrapped all the way around the back of his head. To keep the glasses on his face, Jonathan walked with his nose in the air while he tried to grab food from the line and place it on his tray. He walked to his cabin's table, balancing both the sunglasses and the tray like a juggler. He was facing Skye.

Skye saw a camper at the table reach for the glasses just as Jonathan sat down. Jonathan scowled at the boy and slapped his hand—hard. Skye's eyes searched for Tim, who was busy with another camper's milk that had spilled all over the other end of the table.

"Uh-oh. I smell big trouble," Skye said. "Morgan, watch our kids, will you? We're gonna have a major problem on our hands if someone doesn't get to Jonathan right now."

Skye charged over to Tim's table, watching every move Jonathan and the camper made. Again, the boy reached for the glasses. This time Jonathan gave the boy a shove and then followed up with his trademark gesture—sticking out his tongue. The boy shoved Jonathan back. The glasses flew off Jonathan's face onto the floor. That did it! Jonathan picked up a Styrofoam dish full of pudding, cocked his arm, and prepared to do battle.

"Jonathan! No!" Skye screamed, reaching across the table to stop him.

Splat! Skye took a full dish of chocolate pudding right between the eyes!

Pudding flew everywhere, big globs of it landing on the camper next to Jonathan. The boy picked up his own pudding and threw it. Jonathan ducked, the chocolate splattering all over the shirt of the boy sitting to his right. The boy looked down, started wiping the pudding off, but then grabbed his dish of applesauce. He scowled and took aim.

"Stop it!" Skye screamed.

But no one was listening to Skye. Jonathan picked up his full plate of spaghetti and dumped it right over the head of the boy who had grabbed for his glasses and started the whole mess. At the same time, Jonathan took a full dish of applesauce right on *his* head!

"Food fight!" another boy at the same table yelled.

"Food fight!" the rest of Tim's boys echoed.

In seconds, "Food fight!" rang through the entire cafeteria. Chaos reigned in the large room as chocolate pudding, spaghetti, applesauce, and milk cartons flew everywhere. Buttered bread sailed through the air like Frisbees.

Skye wiped her eyes clear of pudding and looked for Tim.

Splat! A wad of warm spaghetti hit her on the side of her head, clogging her ear. She spotted Tim, who had just taken a glob of pudding in his left eye. She turned to look for Morgan, and a milk carton whizzed by Skye's head. Ducking low, she peeked toward the Five Ferns table.

Above the screams, Skye could hear Morgan yelling, "Stop it, girls! Stop it!" Morgan was waving her hands in front of her, trying to keep the food tide from carrying her away. *Splat!* She took a full plate of spaghetti square in the face.

By this time, the entire room had erupted into loud screams, banging chairs, kids running after one another with plates full of food, and cooks cowering behind the counter.

The staff had lost control and could do nothing but duck. The walls dripped with pudding, and the wagon-wheel chandeliers had been festooned with spaghetti noodles dripping with red sauce.

"Sit down!" Skye wailed, warding off food bullets with her hands.

Splat! Another bomb, cold and gooey, exploded on the back of Skye's head.

"Where's Mr. Wheaten!" she screamed at Tim.

"There!" Tim yelled as he dodged cartons and plates. He pointed at the door.

Mr. Wheaten had just dashed into the room, his eyes bulging at the sight. Quickly he pulled out his whistle. Just as he started to blow it, a pudding bomb exploded in his face. The clogged whistle only sputtered like a fizzling firecracker.

"There's Mr. Wheaten!" some kid in the corner yelled.

As if officially welcoming the director to their party, every camper in the room threw what was left on their plates—or shirts—in Mr. Wheaten's direction. In a mad dash, he scrambled toward the counter where the cooks were hiding. He ducked, but his black Stetson took a blow from a carton of milk and flew into a pool of slop. His silver crew cut peeked above the counter, and this time his whistle let out an earsplitting shriek that bounced off every wall.

In seconds, the place grew as quiet as a graveyard. Was it more from the campers' having nothing to throw than from Mr. Wheaten's whistle?

By now Skye's nerves had her whole body quivering. She reached for a napkin, the only thing she could get her hands on that was clean, and made an effort to wipe her face. Trying to grab a normal breath, she gazed around the room at every staff member and volunteer who was now doing the same. Mr. Wheaten came out from behind the counter, spaghetti and pudding dripping from him like he had been dunked in it. What little showed of his chocolate-covered cheeks flushed bright red.

"All right! Everyone sit down! Right this minute!" he yelled, his hands anchored on his hips. "Staff, get them seated, and go back to your posts!"

Skye started toward her table, sliding on a floor as slippery as ice. She balanced herself, setting chairs upright and helping campers sit. Standing at the end of the Five Ferns table, she glanced at Morgan in her wheel-chair, covered in sauce to match her hair. Her panicky face reflected Skye's feelings exactly.

Skye glanced around the room. Every camper, covered with slop, was sitting in puddles of food on their uprighted chairs. Most were giggling or pointing fingers at others and laughing. Some were crying. The staff members, cloaked with food and embarrassed beyond words, were trying to quiet everyone.

Skye looked for Chad. Busy at a table in the corner, his blond hair was all that she could recognize.

Mr. Wheaten pulled a large red handkerchief from his back jeans pocket and wiped his face. "Now, I want to know, right this minute, who started this!" he barked. He folded his arms and waited.

"He did!" a camper sitting next to Jonathan yelled and pointed. Almost in unison, like a choir perfecting their song, every camper in the room pointed at Jonathan. "He did!" they squealed.

There Jonathan sat, chocolate-covered glasses anchored on his nose, arms folded, and a grin along with his lunch plastered all over his defiant face.

"Tim, bring him to my office! Now!" Mr. Wheaten ordered.

Jonathan, you've done it this time, Skye reasoned. *You are history!*

ounselors," Mr. Wheaten continued, still wiping his face, "I want you to take your campers back to their cabins. All afternoon activities are cancelled. It'll take that long for everybody to get showers. I need one worker from each cabin to get back here as soon as possible to help clean this cafeteria. We'll be shovelin' noodles and puddin' for hours."

On her trek to the Five Ferns cabin, Skye tried to analyze what had just happened. "It really wasn't Jonathan's fault," she said to Morgan. "That other kid provoked him. Jonathan was just trying to tell the kid to leave him alone. But without being able to speak, he acted the only way he knows."

"Well, Tim can't tell Mr. Wheaten that," Morgan said. "His back was turned when the fight started. I'm afraid Jonathan's gonna get shipped out."

"I am too," Skye said. "But this time I'm on his side. Praying for him has changed my mind. I really don't want him to leave."

"What can you do about it?" Morgan wheeled along the walkway in front of the cabin.

"I've got to do something," Skye said. "Let's get these kids cleaned up. Then after I help at the cafeteria, I'll go see Mr. Wheaten."

It was almost suppertime before Skye could slip away to Mr. Wheaten's office. She hurried to the administration building and knocked on his door.

"Come in!" Mr. Wheaten barked.

Skye peeked inside tentatively.

Wearing a fresh western shirt after his unscheduled shower, Mr. Wheaten was just placing the phone down in its cradle. The steer horns above his head, missing the infamous black Stetson, now displayed a beat-up, stained tan cowboy hat. The man's grumpy demeanor from the afternoon's incident dissipated when he saw Skye standing at the door.

"Mr. Wheaten, can we talk?" Skye asked.

"Sure, c'mon in, little lady. I have good news for you. Your worries are over," Mr. Wheaten said. "You were right. Jonathan *is* the Master of Disaster. He'll be gone by tomorrow morning, that is, if I can reach his parents. There's been no answer at their home all afternoon. We aim to help kids here," he said emphatically, "but there's a limit to what we can do. This kid's got to go."

Skye made her way to a chair in front of the desk and sat down. "That's why I'm here," she said. "This time it wasn't his fault."

Mr. Wheaten's eyebrows shot up like he had just heard the tallest tale this side of Texas. "Now, Annie, you ain't tryin' to hog-tie me, are you? I should think you'd be the first one in line to wave good-bye."

"No, it's the truth," Skye said. "I saw the whole thing. The kid sitting next to him started it by grabbing for his sunglasses. Jonathan just wanted to be left alone, but the other camper wouldn't stop."

Mr. Wheaten leaned back in his chair and placed his hands behind his head. "Well, why didn't Tim tell me this?"

"Tim didn't see what happened with Jonathan. He was busy with a kid who had spilled his milk."

Mr. Wheaten, deep in thought, rubbed his chin. "I see. Maybe the Lord didn't want me to get through to Jonathan's parents."

Skye leaned forward, placing her hands on Mr. Wheaten's desk. "I've been praying an awful lot for Jonathan lately. Please give him one more chance. I'm willing to keep trying."

"Well, if you're willing, little lady, then I'm willing," Mr. Wheaten said with a big smile. "Let's go find Jonathan and tell him."

❀❀❀

After supper, Skye took her weekly furlough when she had several hours all to herself. The campers and most of the staff had gone to the gymnasium. There the owner and curator of central Pennsylvania's Jungleland was putting on a display of exotic birds and snakes. Wild animals fascinated Skye, but she decided to ride Champ bareback around the deserted campgrounds. *I need time to think and pray*, she told herself as she trotted Champ around the barn and headed toward the lake.

Approaching the swimming pool, Skye saw the boys' locker room door opening. Backing out, Chad was busy wrestling with a mop and a sloshing bucket on wheels. Skye could tell that he had just finished sanitizing the room.

"I sure hope he doesn't see me," Skye whispered to Champ. She leaned forward, patted his neck, and looked the other way as the horse clip-clopped past the pool. "He's probably entertaining Linda with his mop," she whispered again.

"Hey! Skye!" Chad yelled.

"Oh, no," Skye said to Champ. "I can't face him yet. Not after what happened yesterday."

"Skye! Over here!" Chad turned his volume up a notch.

Skye slowed Champ to a walk, straightened her back like a soldier at attention, and looked nonchalantly toward Chad. Feigning surprise, she yelled, "Oh—Chad—hi there!"

"Wait a minute!" he yelled, throwing the mop against the door. He charged out the open pool gate to Skye. "Do you have a minute?" he said in short breaths. "I have something I need to talk to you about."

Skye looked into Chad's brown eyes, and her heart started to melt. Then she remembered Linda. "Well, I only have an hour left of furlough. I need to take a ride and do some thinking and praying," she said coldly.

"But Skye, this is important," Chad said. He glanced toward the lake. "How about we take a walk down there?"

For the first time since she had seen Linda and Chad together, Skye found herself saying yes to Chad. She slid off Champ's back and started leading him toward the lake. After Chad locked the gate to the pool, he rejoined Skye.

"So, what's up?" Skye looked straight ahead. *He probably wants to tell me he's marrying Linda.*

"Well, for one thing," Chad said, "I wanted to know if you had survived the last twenty-four hours. It looks like you did. You've had it rough with that Jonathan kid. They said he started the food fight at lunchtime. What a mess!"

"Yeah, I'm okay," Skye said in a softer tone. "I've been doin' an awful lot of praying about Jonathan. He's a very lonely kid. And by the way, Chad, he didn't start that food fight. The camper next to him did."

"No kidding! So Jonathan's not getting shipped out?"

"No. And I'm glad."

"Yeah, I am too. Everybody deserves another chance."

"I sure know about that," Skye said.

With Champ following, Chad and Skye meandered down the sloping lawn beside the waterslide. A brilliant sunset gave the lake and surrounding woods a deep pink cast. If it weren't for Linda, Skye would have thought she was walking in a dream.

At the water's edge, Chad pulled a shoot of tall grass from a cluster of weeds and stuck it between his teeth. Skye dropped Champ's reins, allowing him to feast on the succulent, moist grass on the shore. Skye picked up several flat stones and skipped them across the water. *It doesn't get any better than this*, Skye thought. *Almost.*

"So what did you want to tell me?" she asked Chad while skipping the stones.

"Skye, I've always considered you one of my best friends, so I want to run something by you. Tell me what you think."

Skye walked back to Champ and stroked his neck. "Okay, what?" she said defensively.

"You know, the guest speakers at camp have given some mighty good sermons. And—well—the Lord's been speaking to my heart. I think he wants me to go into the ministry, maybe as a missionary or a youth pastor or something."

Skye's eyebrows peaked, and she quickly tried to wipe the surprise off her face. "So this isn't about Linda?"

"What would Linda have to do with *my* future?" Chad scratched his head. "Anyway, what do you think? Would I make a good preacher or missionary? You know me about as well as any of the kids at Madison, or at church."

Skye stared into the face of a young man whose eyes pleaded for an answer. Her own face flushed hot, then she turned toward Champ and stroked his soft, velvety nose. "Yeah, Chad, I think you'd make a great preacher. I mean, you're so good with people. And your music would be a big plus. Yeah, you'd be great. I'm sure you would." She looked back at Chad and smiled.

"Well, you're one of the few people who know about this," he said almost in a whisper. "I told Linda, and I called my best friend back home and told him."

Linda, Linda, Linda! I am so sick of hearing that name! Skye fumed. *I've got to get this straight, right now.* "While we're on the topic of Linda," Skye interjected, "I need to know something right now, Chad Dressler."

"Sure, Skye Nicholson. But you look so serious. What is it?" His dimples dissolved into a devilish smile.

"What is it with you and Linda? I mean, I see you together everywhere. She's—like—your shadow!"

"What does that have to do with anything? We've always been close."

"Yeah! Very close!" Skye growled.

"Well," Chad said while he chewed on the grass, "she is special to me. And she'd be special to you if you were in my shoes!"

"What on earth do you mean, 'If I were in your shoes'?"

"Skye, I don't have a sister. Linda's my only girl cousin. We've always been close. She's like the sister I've never had but wished I did."

hat?" Skye's mouth dropped open.

"Now, Skye, don't act so surprised."

"Your cousin? Linda's your—your cousin?"

"Well, sure. Always was and always will be. I thought you knew that."

"How would I know that, Chad Dressler?"

"Don't you remember when she visited from New York a few years back and she came to the youth retreat at Keystone Stables?"

"Chad, a few years back?"

"Oh, that's right, you weren't living there at the time, were you?"

"No," Skye said, her face frozen in shock. "I thought you—she—she always calls you 'honey'!"

Chad's dimpled smile made his eyes sparkle. "Aw, so that's why you've been acting so funny. You thought we were—" He let loose a hearty laugh. "Skye, I thought you knew me better than that. Girlfriends aren't in my plans until I'm much older. Linda has called me 'honey' since we were little kids. It's a family joke. We both got in trouble one time when we ate a whole jar of honey and got sick. Since then she always reminds me of that dumb trick by calling me 'honey.' That's all it means."

Skye felt like the biggest fool at Camp Oneega. Maybe even in the whole wide world. Her face flushed hot again, mostly from embarrassment. "I—I'm sorry, Chad. I just read the whole thing wrong."

"Forget it," Chad said, his face growing sincere, "and I'll let you in on a little secret. When I'm ready for a girl-friend, you'll be the first one on the list."

The next few days Skye floated on air. Linda was Chad's cousin? It was too good to be true. With Linda no longer a major source of irritation, Skye focused on helping the Problem Child of Camp Oneega.

Every morning, she met Jonathan at the riding corral where he was learning how to saddle and bridle Buddy, how to clean his hooves, and how to apply bug juice. The boy had advanced in his riding lessons to where he was now ready to learn how to trot Buddy in the corral. Today it was time for another lesson. Skye and Champ stood next to Jonathan and Buddy, ready to begin.

"Okay, Jonathan," Skye signed, "mount Buddy. I want you to walk him around the corral one time in each direction. Then come back here, and we'll work on trotting."

Jonathan smiled, pulled his helmet strap tighter under his chin, and nudged Buddy forward. Flawlessly, he walked Buddy as he had been instructed. Then he came back to Skye.

"Very good," Skye signed. "Now we're going to learn to trot. I'm going to trot Champ around the corral. You sit here and watch. Okay?"

"Okay," Jonathan signed.

Skye mounted Champ and rode him around the corral one time, stopping in front of her watchful student. "I'll do it once more," she signed. "You watch my balance and my feet. Also, look at how little I pull on the reins. Okay?"

"Okay," he signed.

Again Skye trotted around and stopped in front of Jonathan.

"Now, you try it. Remember, don't pull back hard on the reins. And don't kick him. Just rub his belly with your heels. Buddy will respond."

"Okay." Jonathan smiled. He started, first in a walk, then in a proper trot. But halfway around the corral, he started pushing his weight forward in the stirrups and lifting himself out of the saddle every other beat of Buddy's trot.

"He's posting!" Skye said with no one listening. "Jonathan!" she screamed.

Shifting his weight forward, Jonathan sent Buddy into a full canter. The boy yanked the reins to the side, turning the horse into the center of the corral. Buddy came to an abrupt and confused stop.

Skye raced Champ into the center of the corral, coming to a sliding stop next to Buddy. Panic filled Buddy's eyes as he sidestepped, fighting the tight hold Jonathan had on the bit. Skye reached down and grabbed the horse's bridle, attempting to settle him down.

"Jonathan, relax the reins!" she signed. "You don't post when you ride Western style. Buddy has no clue what you're doing."

"I always ride like that!" Jonathan signed.

"Only because you learned English style on an English-trained horse. Now listen! All these horses at the camp are trained *Western*."

"No," Jonathan chopped the air. "I don't like this way." He started pulling Buddy to the side.

Skye grabbed Buddy's bridle again and calmed him down. "Jonathan, you *will not* post with Buddy. Your lesson is done!"

Jonathan pouted for several seconds and stared at Skye. Then, dropping the reins on the saddle's horn, he started to cry. He ripped off his riding helmet, threw it on the ground, and jumped off his horse. Wailing like someone had just given him a black eye, Jonathan fled into the barn.

Now what! Skye said to herself. She reached over to Buddy's saddle, grabbed his reins, and led him back toward the barn. Tying both horses' reins to the corral posts, Skye ran into the barn after Jonathan. Over in a dark corner filled with hay bales, Jonathan sat, crying his eyes out.

Skye hurried to kneel in front of Jonathan.

Venturing one nasty look at Skye, the boy lowered his head onto his folded arms. He sobbed and sobbed.

Skye touched him, and Jonathan pulled away fiercely. He pivoted his body a half turn, completely ignoring Skye. The battle of the wills had begun again.

"More trouble?" Skye heard Mr. Wheaten's voice coming from the open barn door.

"Yes," she answered. "He wouldn't listen during his riding lesson again."

"Need any help?" Mr. Wheaten asked.

"I think I can handle this one," she said. "Thanks anyway."

"I'll be in the corral if you need me." The man's voice trailed away.

Skye sat on her haunches, contemplating her next move. Jonathan stared off into space with crocodile tears streaming out of his big brown eyes. By now, his nose had joined in, thick liquid running down over his lips.

Skye reached into her jeans pocket for a wad of tissues. All in one move, she pulled one loose and reached toward Jonathan's nose.

Smack! Jonathan slapped Skye's hand so hard the tissue flew. With eyes full of contempt and the nastiest scowl he could muster, he stared straight at her.

"I hate you!" he signed viciously.

Favoring her stinging hand, Skye sat dumbfounded. "You don't mean that," she signed. "You always say you like me."

"I don't like you!" he said. "I hate you! Just leave me alone!" Again he turned, this time with his back toward Skye. He buried his face in his arms, and again cried in loud sobs.

Slowly Skye stood, and for a brief moment stared at the heartbroken boy. *He hates me.*

The last time she had heard those awful words was in one of her foster homes, a long time ago, where she lived above a garage and was treated like a maid. The other kids in that home had said that too. At that terrible place, she knew she wasn't wanted, spending more time in the garage than in the house. Ugly memories filled her mind like a flooding cesspool. Her own eyes filled with tears.

Should I try to help? she asked herself. *Can I?* She reached and almost touched Jonathan's quivering shoulder but quickly withdrew her hand.

I'm not helping him at all, she told herself. *I'm only making things worse.* With her own tears streaming, Skye turned and fled the barn.

"Skye!" Mr. Wheaten yelled from behind. "Wait!"

Halfway across the road, Skye stopped. Wiping her eyes, she turned as Mr. Wheaten covered the distance.

"What's the matter? Are you hurt?" Mr. Wheaten's eyes and opened hands expressed his deep concern.

Skye's body heaved with deep sobs. "Oh, Mr. Wheaten, I just can't help Jonathan. He hates me. I just can't do this anymore."

"Aw, little lady," the big man said. He reached his muscular arms around Skye and drew her toward him. He patted her on the head. "That's all right, Annie. You've done the best you could."

"But—but I don't want to disappoint you—or the Lord!" she cried, wiping her nose on her arm.

"Oh, you haven't," Mr. Wheaten said in a consoling voice. "I think you just need a rest from all this pressure. Don't feel so bad. I'll reassign Jonathan and his classes to Tim and Linda. Maybe my wife can help too. Now don't you worry your pretty little head over this. We'll help this kid yet."

Skye stepped back from the man and stared into his compassionate eyes. "But I can't! And I wanted to help him. I feel like such a failure!"

"Well, now, the summer's just startin'. You can work with him again, if you want to. Maybe in a week or two, you'll feel strong enough to try it. What do ya say?"

Skye pulled a tissue from her pocket and wiped her nose. "If you say so, Mr. Wheaten. This might be the best thing for all of us, especially Jonathan."

Mr. Wheaten looked around and then focused on the barn. "Is he still in there?"

"Yeah." Skye sniffled.

"You tend to the horses," Mr. Wheaten said. "I'll get Tim, and we'll take care of Jonathan. Sooner or later, he's gotta learn to listen."

"I sure hope it's not later," Skye said, walking toward the corral.

"Me too, little lady," Mr. Wheaten said. "Me too."

chapter thirteen

The next morning in the cafeteria, Skye and Morgan monitored their girls at the Five Ferns table. Caleb had just gotten Morgan her tray and was sitting beside her. Skye sat down at the other end of the table and searched the room, looking for a certain blond young man. At a corner table Chad and Linda sat together, laughing up a storm. Skye just smiled.

At the doorway Tim's boys came in and headed toward the breakfast line. Skye noticed that worry shrouded Tim's face. After he scanned the room, he rushed toward her table.

"Skye, have you seen Jonathan?" His voice conveyed raw panic.

"No," she said, confused. "I only see him this time of the day when he comes in here with your group. And besides, I'm not working with him anymore. At least, not for the time being." She too quickly scanned the room.

Tim's rambling words betrayed his growing concern. "I thought maybe he had come in here ahead of our scheduled time. When I woke the boys up this morning, his bed was empty. I thought he was in the bathroom. I

83

know now that I should have checked. I got so busy I forgot about him. Later, after everybody was dressed, I lined up the boys to bring them for breakfast, but he wasn't there. I checked the bathroom then, but he wasn't there either. Now I'm really worried."

"It sounds to me like he might be pulling one of his neat little bathroom tricks again," Skye said confidently.

"What do you mean?" Tim asked.

"He sits on top of the toilet against the wall and pulls his feet up. Then you can't see if he's in any of the stalls." Skye stood, directing her words to Morgan. "I've got to see if Jonathan's up in his cabin. I'll be right back."

"Do you want me to come with you?" Tim asked.

"Nah," Skye said, already heading toward the door. "You get your boys settled. They need you. I'll find Jonathan."

"Yeah," Morgan said, "our girls are already settled. We'll be cool, won't we, girls?"

"Yeah, cool," they said, one after another.

Skye hurried out of the mess hall and ran past the barn to the boys' cabins all facing the pool. Rushing into Tim's cabin, she headed straight to the bathroom. Quickly she went to three stalls and pushed on the doors, fully expecting one to be locked. But all three doors swung open freely.

In a heartbeat, the panic she had seen on Tim's face raced through her veins like a charge of electricity.

She ran back to the cafeteria where Tim and Mr. Wheaten stood talking near the food line. As soon as Skye hurried in, their anxious looks turned in her direction.

"He's not there!" Skye said when she joined them.

"Now where could that boy be?" Mr. Wheaten raised his hat and scratched his head. "He seemed all right when we talked to him yesterday." He glanced at Skye. "All I wanted him to do was apologize to you some time today. That didn't seem to bother him much at all."

"Yeah," Tim added, "and you certainly weren't mean to him, Mr. Wheaten. But remember, all Jonathan kept saying was 'Okay.' Maybe he didn't really understand what we wanted him to do."

"It's awfully hard to tell what a deaf kid really understands," Skye said. "They nod their heads 'yes' all the time, even when they don't have a clue what we're talking about. They really have it rough."

Mr. Wheaten squared his hat on his head and took a deep breath. "Well, we've got to find him—and now!" He walked to the sound system and picked up the microphone. "Attention, ladies and gentlemen. May I have your attention?"

The room settled to not even a whisper.

Mr. Wheaten continued. "Jonathan Martin did not come in here with his cabin. Has anyone seen him this morning?"

"No!" echoed across the room. Dozens of campers shook their heads.

"All right then," Mr. Wheaten said. "I'm going to check with the sick bay and the maintenance crew. Maybe somebody has seen him wandering around. If not, staff and volunteers, we need to put Emergency Plan A into action. You who are members of the search team, please meet me in my office in ten minutes." He placed the microphone down and hurried outside.

As instructed, in ten minutes the search team assembled at Mr. Wheaten's desk. Skye, Chad, Linda, and Tim were among the eight who eagerly awaited the next orders.

Mr. Wheaten stood under his steer horns with worry plastered all over his face. "Nobody, and I mean nobody, has seen Jonathan today. I want you people to scour these grounds. Leave no rock unturned. And look up in every tree. Kids his size love to climb trees! Linda, you take the swimming pool, slide, and pond area. Tim, you check all the cabins, boys' and girls', and the picnic area. Chad, take an ATV and go down to the lower east end of the camp. Check the playing fields, including all the equipment, and then search the perimeter of the whole camp. It's gonna take you a while to cover ten acres, but take your time and be thorough. Skye, I want you to check the corral area and barn, including the tack room and hayloft. The rest of you come with me. I'll take you by truck to the outskirts of the camp. We'll check each hiking trail leading away from the camp for half a mile or so. I sure hope he hasn't wandered off into the woods. It'll be like searching for a penny in a copper mine."

"What'll we do if we find him?" Chad asked.

"Bring him right back here, even if you have to drag him." Mr. Wheaten raised his finger emphatically. "This is no joke, even if he thinks it's funny. We'll all meet back here in an hour, with or without him. Oh, and before you all go, let's have a word of prayer."

After Mr. Wheaten prayed for the searchers and Jonathan, everyone left the office in a rush.

Skye hurried across the street toward the barn. Sliding the door open, she went inside. First, she checked the hay bales on ground level where twice in as many weeks Jonathan had hidden to pout.

No Jonathan.

She ran to the large tack room at the other end of the barn, searching under and behind barrels, saddles, blankets, and anything large enough to hide a skinny little kid.

No Jonathan.

She ran up the stairs to the hayloft where she looked behind hundreds of bales stacked like gigantic blocks.

No Jonathan.

Down the stairs she flew. She searched every stall on both sides of the long corridor. She glanced at her watch. An hour had just about passed.

"Champ," she said when she got to her horse's stall, "I have no time to socialize right now. Jonathan's on the run—again!"

Champ nickered and nodded as Skye hurried past. She finished checking the rest of the stalls and headed toward the sliding door.

Wait! Skye stopped dead in her tracks.

"That last stall is Buddy's stall!" she said. "And it's empty!"

She hurried back and leaned over the Dutch door, scanning the stall like Buddy just *had* to be in it. A layer of straw bedding and one pile of horse manure were all she saw.

Rushing in, she bent down and touched a lump of manure. Cold and dry. "That means he hasn't been in here for hours!" she told herself.

She darted out of the stall and ran back down the long corridor. Stopping at the doorway of the tack room, she zeroed in on the far left corner, at the brace and hook where Buddy's saddle and bridle belonged.

Empty!

"Oh, no!" Skye yelled. "That means—he's ridden off the campgrounds!"

※ ※ ※

At 10:00 a.m., Skye sat on Champ outside the barn. Mr. Wheaten and four other staff members were sitting on horseback as well. Every rider held an open map. All the saddles had been equipped with a canteen of water, a first-aid kit, and a blanket rolled up on the back. From each rider's belt, a cell phone dangled from one side and a megaphone from the other. Mr. Wheaten was giving last-minute instructions to the search team.

"Our job is to comb this immediate area," he said, his voice ladened with stress. "Caleb and two other men are already searching the main highway and the woods on the other side of the road. I've notified the Shamokin Park Rangers, and four of them have started to search their six hundred acres on ATVs. It's up to us to cover the north, south, and east woods adjoining the camp. Thank goodness we have blue skies. That will make the job much easier."

"Do we have to stay in pairs?" Tim asked.

Skye and Chad exchanged smiles.

"Yes, safety first!" Mr. Wheaten answered. "Besides, if Jonathan is hurt, he'll need all the help he can get. Any other questions before we head out?"

"What about wild animals?" An anxious look swept over Chad's face. "I mean, could Jonathan be in any danger?"

Mr. Wheaten squared his hat and forced a smile that belied the worry eating away inside. "Bear and cougar have been sighted in these woods. So, yes, I would say there is some concern. However, as long as they're not provoked, they'd probably run in the opposite direction from any human. Also, the tweeter on your megaphones will do a number on any animal. Set that high-pitched noise off, and they'll hightail it into the next county. Don't forget, that whistle will bring Buddy right to you if he's within hearing range."

Skye squared her own Stetson and stroked Champ's neck. "What if we don't find him? You said yourself that there are hundreds of acres to cover and dozens of hiking trails."

"We have to find him," Mr. Wheaten declared, "and God will help us. I've already notified the state police, and if we don't find the boy by nightfall, they'll activate a missing persons APB at daybreak. In addition to an army of volunteers from nearby towns, the police will use their own search teams and helicopter as well."

"What about Jonathan's parents?" another rider asked. "Do they know?"

"I called them about an hour ago," Mr. Wheaten said. "Of course, they're frantic. They should arrive here some time in the late afternoon. I only hope by then Jonathan can greet them."

"Mr. Wheaten," Skye asked, "can we pray before we start?"

"By all means, little lady," he answered. "God knows exactly where Jonathan and Buddy are."

Mr. Wheaten prayed. Tugging the brim of his hat down, he said, "Remember, stay together, and don't get lost yourselves. Use your cell phones to keep in touch with one another. If you see any signs that Jonathan has been where you are, let us know. And Skye and Chad, you've got a tough job. Along the stream to Oneega Falls, at least a dozen trails shoot off from the main one. The dampness from the stream makes the footing treacherous, even for the horses. Be very careful. Any other questions?"

"No," everyone responded.

"Then let's synchronize our watches," Mr. Wheaten said, glancing at his. "It's ten fifteen. We'll meet back here in five hours. Let's move out."

chapter fourteen

Five hours later, Skye and Chad joined Tim and the rest of the search team back at the barn. No one had seen a trace of Jonathan. The riders dismounted with heads hung low. Hardly a word was spoken.

Despite her love for riding, Skye was glad to slip off Champ's back. Her body ached, and she was sure her legs would stay bowed forever. A lather of sweat coated Champ as he huffed from his grueling hike. Skye petted his dilating nose and kissed him on his sweaty cheek. "Good boy, Champ," she said. "You get double oats for supper tonight."

Lined up at the corral fence, a new team of six staff members sat on fresh horses. After Skye, Chad, and Tim relinquished their equipment, they joined the rest of their team in the corral to cool down the horses. Mr. Wheaten started to address the fresh riders, ready to search until dark.

"And remember," he said, his exhausted voice wavering, "start heading back here by eight o'clock. I don't want anyone else lost in the woods. One is bad enough!"

"Mr. Wheaten!" Skye heard his secretary yell from the doorway of the office across the street. "The Martins are here!"

"Be right there!" he yelled back.

"I'm certainly glad I am not Mr. Wheaten," Skye said to Chad and Tim as they walked their horses. "How do you tell people that their son is lost in hundreds of acres of woods?"

"That is a tough one," Chad said. "There's no easy way to say it. He sure needs our prayers right about now."

"Especially since it wasn't his fault. I feel like it's my fault all the way around. I shouldn't have gotten so angry with that kid. It's my fault. I know it is."

"Skye, it's nobody's fault but Jonathan's," Tim said. "He just needs—well—he needs a lot of love and under-standing, but he also has to learn that he can't have his own way all the time. You were only trying to teach him what is right. Now don't feel so bad."

"Skye and Tim!" Mr. Wheaten yelled as the fresh team started moving out. "Would you please come with me? You can explain Jonathan's behavior over the last two weeks and what led up to his running away."

"Oh, no," Skye said to Chad. "It looks like I *am* gonna find out what it's like to be Mr. Wheaten."

"I think right now all he needs is some moral support," Chad said. "Give me Champ. I'll finish cooling him down. You'll do fine."

"Thanks, Chad," Skye said, handing him the reins. "I just can't imagine what those parents must be going through."

Skye and Tim joined Mr. Wheaten, and the three headed toward the office. Mr. Wheaten walked at an obvious slow pace. He squared his hat, tugging it down as though he were in a slow-motion film. His tired face said it all. He dreaded the next few moments.

For once, Skye found it easy to keep up with Mr. Wheaten's stride. Was it because he walked so slowly or because her heart was pounding like a drum?

What can we possibly say to make Jonathan's parents feel better? Skye pondered. *Nothing*, she concluded. *Nothing at all.*

Inside, Mr. Wheaten made awkward introductions through a veil of fake smiles, and everyone sat in a semicircle in front of his desk. In no mood to flip his Stetson onto the horn, Mr. Wheaten dropped his hat on top of a pile of papers and flopped into his chair.

Skye's glance darted around the room, focusing at last on Mr. and Mrs. Martin. The woman's puffy and bloodshot eyes exuded pain from her round face, but the man's thin frame and balding head were fixed in a demeanor of cool indifference. The obvious tension between the two chilled the whole room.

Mr. Wheaten began. "Folks, I'm not going to start by making excuses. We're just awfully sorry this happened. But I promise you, we will find him. We have a search team out there right now."

Tears trickled down from Mrs. Martin's red eyes. "But how could this happen? Don't your people watch these children all the time?"

Mr. Wheaten pointed at Tim. "Tim was the last one to see Jonathan, last night."

Tim nodded at the Martins. "When lights went out at 10:00 p.m., Jonathan was in his bed. I made two more checks, at one and at four. He was in bed then too."

"We figure Jonathan must have slipped out around six, saddled his horse, and then took off before anyone saw him," Mr. Wheaten said. "I assure you, this has never happened before. I'm sorry to have to say this, but Jonathan has not been very cooperative."

Skye crossed her legs and tried to relax, but her voice squeaked with stress. "I've been working with Jonathan for two weeks, and he just wouldn't listen. Everything I tried to show him in the riding corral, he did the opposite."

"You're telling me!" Mr. Martin said. "He won't listen to a thing I say to him."

Mrs. Martin dabbed a tissue at her cheeks and looked straight ahead, almost away from her husband. "Maybe that's because you don't talk to him. You've never even learned sign language. How do you think that makes Jonathan feel?"

"I don't need to know sign language. You can do all that. I'm his father, and all I need to do is provide for the boy. And I have done that above and beyond the call of duty. He has everything a kid his age would want."

Mr. Wheaten leaned forward, folding his hands on his desk. "Mr. Martin, your son is a troubled child, but not because he's deaf. He needs you. He needs you to love and understand him."

"I do," Mr. Martin said unconvincingly.

Mrs. Martin turned and stared her husband square in the eye. "Oh, really? So you love and understand him? When's the last time you took him on a trip—or to a park? You've never even taken him for an ice-cream cone. He's your son too!"

Mr. Martin's face turned bright red. He pursed his lips, ready to lash out at his wife. Instead, he stood abruptly and walked around to the back of his chair, then leaned on it. "Maybe that's because you never let him out of your sight," he said sternly. "It's a miracle you ever agreed to send him to school or away to this camp for the summer."

"Mr. and Mrs. Martin—please!" Mr. Wheaten said. "Your child is lost out there in the woods. This is no time to be airing family differences. We all need to band together for Jonathan."

As Skye sat staring at these two people doing battle, her heart sank to the bottoms of her feet. *Their son is missing*, she thought as her eyes flooded with tears, *and all they can do is fight? They could have so much more. I must tell them.*

"Mr. Wheaten"—Skye raised her finger—"could I please say something?"

"Sure, little lady," Mr. Wheaten said, sliding back into his chair and folding his arms. "Go right ahead."

"Mr. and Mrs. Martin, it's very clear that you're not together at all on how to help Jonathan. I think that's what's bothering him. He can't hear what you're saying at home, but he sure can see your faces and how you act toward each other. He probably thinks it's all his fault."

Mr. Martin's face reddened again. His knuckles turned white as he gripped the back of his chair tighter. "Young lady, I don't believe that's any concern of yours."

"Oh, but Skye knows where she's comin' from," Mr. Wheaten said. "She's been through an awful lot in her thirteen years."

Tim leaned forward in his chair. "Yeah, I think she really knows how Jonathan feels."

"How can she know?" Mr. Martin said in a sarcastic tone. "She's not deaf!"

"No," Skye said, "but I've been in at least a dozen foster homes, and I think I know where Jonathan's coming from. Some foster parents gave me all kinds of things, but they never gave me the love I wanted—needed. In a few other foster homes, I just felt like I was in the way. All I wanted to do was run."

"But then she met Tom and Eileen Chambers, her foster parents now," Mr. Wheaten said.

"And I also met Christ," Skye said, her teary eyes darting back and forth between the Martins. "When Mom and Dad Chambers shared the love of God with me, it changed me. I don't want to run anymore. Have you shared the love of God with your son?"

Silence.

Tears trickled down Mrs. Martin's face. She hung her head and dabbed at her eyes and nose.

Skye looked at Mr. Martin, who was staring back as though someone had just punched him in the nose. In deep thought, he slowly sat down next to his wife. He looked at Skye, his eyes turning red and watery. "No, I haven't," he whispered. "I haven't shared much of anything with my son, least of all God or myself."

"Well, folks," Mr. Wheaten said, "we're trusting in God that it's not too late, for your son or you. Somewhere out there is a mighty lonely little kid. He needs you two, now more than ever. He needs undivided attention from you, sir, and discipline from you, ma'am. Together, you and God can turn this boy around."

Mr. Martin turned to his wife. "I'm so sorry," he said.

"I am too," Mrs. Martin said, sobbing. "I hope it's not too late."

Standing, Mr. Wheaten picked up the phone. "Let's get you two settled in one of our guesthouses. But before we do, let's have a word of prayer. God *is* in charge over this whole situation, and he can make it right."

Mr. Martin wiped the corners of his eyes like he was flicking away dirt. "I don't know why it took me so long to realize how I had hurt my boy. Thanks, Skye, for sharing your story. If God gives me another chance with my son, things will be different." With a smile, he reached toward Skye and warmly shook her hand.

Mrs. Martin looked up, tears streaming down her face. "Things will be different with me too." Reaching over toward her husband, she smiled and grasped his open hand.

chapter fifteen

At dawn, Skye again positioned Champ in a horse lineup outside the barn. Jonathan had now been missing for twenty-four hours. Overhead, a helicopter chopped the air, already searching the woods. Volunteers from nearby fire companies were scouring the Shamokin State Park within a five-mile radius of Camp Oneega. Skye and her search team checked their gear and prepared to comb the trails around the camp one more time.

Mr. Wheaten mounted his horse and squared his hat. "It doesn't matter if you have to backtrack over ground that's already been covered. Some of these trails intertwine for miles. This time take a good, hard look at any bluffs, high and low. There are a half dozen hollowed-out rocks and caves where Jonathan could have sought shelter overnight."

"Mr. Wheaten?" Skye couldn't help interrupting.

"Yes, little lady?"

"Chad and I covered the area up by Oneega Falls yesterday, but I'd really like to check it out again. It seems to me that Jonathan would want to go somewhere he's been before. Just last week he was at the falls campsite."

"Good point," Mr. Wheaten said.

Chad pulled his horse alongside Champ. "Mr. Wheaten, we didn't have enough time to check every corner of the campsite on foot. Didn't you tell us there are trails that lead away from the top of the falls?"

"Yes, indeedy," Mr. Wheaten said.

"Well, we never got that far yesterday," Skye said. "Today we'll make sure we cover those."

Mr. Wheaten tugged the brim of his hat down firmly. "Fine. Thank the Lord we've had warm weather. Jonathan will be mighty hungry, but at least he won't suffer from exposure. I want you all to blast your tweeters every ten minutes. Buddy will pick up that sound even if he's half a mile away from you. Any other questions?" he asked everyone.

"No," they all answered.

"Remember teams, keep in touch by phone, especially if you see anything that looks like Jonathan has been where you are. We've got to find him soon. Even though we've got sunny skies now, the weather forecast calls for severe thunderstorms later today. Lightning in these thick woods is no laughing matter. If you hear thunder, even if it's in the distance, you all head back here on the double."

"Yes, sir!" they all yelled.

"Be back here at 11:00 a.m. or before, depending on the weather. Let's move out!"

Skye and Chad wasted no time riding past the lake and heading up the trail to Oneega Falls. Every ten minutes, they stopped to tweet a megaphone. They climbed the mountainside, checking and rechecking every trail for several hundred yards on both sides of the main trek.

Nearing the wooden bridge right below the falls, Skye glanced at her watch. "Three hours already gone!" she said more to herself than to Chad. A sharp breeze whisked through the ravine, sending the treetops into a frantic dance. Skye looked up at a sea of dark, fast-moving clouds. Under her tied-down Stetson, her hair blew wildly.

"Chad, look at those clouds," she said. "Those thunderstorms can't be too far away."

"Those clouds spell nothing but trouble. We better keep moving." Chad squared his hat tightly.

The two of them rode their horses across the bridge and brought them to a stop. A rush of colder air shook the trees around them. Again, Chad studied the sky. "This is definitely not good."

Skye's cell phone rang.

"Hello, Skye speaking."

"Annie, this is Mr. Wheaten. I don't like the looks of those clouds. Keep an eye on them. At the first sound of thunder, you two head back."

"We will, sir. Over and out," she said in a brief attempt to lighten the mood.

"Was that Mr. Wheaten?" Chad asked.

"Yep. He's warning everyone to watch the weather."

"We're too close now to turn back. Let's check the campsite."

"Good idea." Skye glanced down at the banks on each side of the bridge. "Remember what happened here with Jonathan last week?"

"How could I forget!" Chad moaned.

"That kid sure is — hey — Chad, look down there, on the left bank."

"Where?"

"There. Next to that cluster of pebbles." Skye jumped off Champ and ran down to the water's edge. She picked up an object from the mud and wiped it on her jeans. "Chad, look! Jonathan's big sunglasses! He was here!"

"But when?" Chad grabbed the megaphone. He pushed the tweeter button and let out three long, high-pitched blasts. Then he phoned Mr. Wheaten.

Skye ran back up the bank and mounted Champ. "He's got to be somewhere near here. I just know it."

"C'mon," Chad said. "Let's check the campsite."

Prodding their mounts carefully, Skye and Chad hurried on down the treacherous trail. As they rounded the last bluff before the falls, a black horse trotted right up to them and stopped.

"Buddy!" Skye yelled.

"But where's Jonathan!" Chad said.

Skye grabbed the horse's dangling reins. Tying them into a knot, she reached over and slipped them around the horn of Buddy's saddle. "Okay, boy, now it's time for you to use that special training. Take us to Jonathan."

"Where is he, Buddy?" Chad said.

"Chad, listen!"

Rumble, rumble rolled the distant thunder. Another wisp of wind chilled the air.

"Let's go, Buddy," Skye said.

Buddy turned, backtracking on the trail. Crossing the gravel shoreline in front of the falls, he continued toward the bluff that hid the campsite. But he didn't stop there. Squeezing his way through a narrow opening between towering pine trees and gigantic boulders, he doubled back behind the falls on a pathway of slippery stones. Staying close to the black horse, Skye's and Chad's mounts followed.

"Where's he going?" Skye asked. "I didn't even know this trail was here."

"I wonder if Mr. Wheaten knows about this one," Chad said.

Carefully, the horses made their way on the slippery path.

Rumble, rumble. Another roll of thunder sent a faint warning, despite the competing, nearly deafening roar of the falls.

"The storm is getting much closer!" Chad yelled as he scanned the clouds again.

"We've got to keep going!" Skye's voice could scarcely be heard. "Jonathan's got to be here somewhere! He's got to be!"

At a snail's pace, Buddy led them through a narrow crevasse to the side of the towering falls. Skye's eyes widened as she studied the scene before her. A flood of powerful water tumbled from the shelf of rocks high above. The ground trembled from the roar of the falls crashing just below. Skye stood in her stirrups, her eyes scouring the area for any sign of Jonathan. She spotted an opening behind the falls, a hollowed-out rock formation large enough to park a truck.

"Chad, look! Behind the falls!" Skye dismounted. "Pray that Jonathan's in there. Get Mr. Wheaten on the phone and tell him where we are. I'll check it out!"

Chad was already pushing cell phone buttons. "Skye, be careful."

Gingerly, Skye balanced herself on the next few feet of slippery stones that led behind the falls. Billows of mist filled the compact space like fast-moving fog. She stopped to listen, and a shiver charged through her as droplets covered her like a wet blanket. No sound, not even thunder, could now penetrate the deafening crash of the falls. *If Buddy was here yesterday, I understand why he didn't hear our tweeters*, she said to herself.

Skye searched every dark corner as she slid along the humongous hollowed-out rock. Suddenly, her heart pounded like a drum, her whole body racked with its beat. She stopped and stared into the darkness. *Wild animals could be lurking in this black hole*, she warned herself.

There! Off to the side! Something! Or could it be someone lying in a curled-up ball?

Skye inched forward. Studying the form. Hoping. Searching the shadows. Listening.

One more brave step forward and—

"Jonathan! I found him, Chad! He's in here! Can you hear me?"

"Yes! Just barely! I'll phone Mr. Wheaten again, and I'll be right there!"

Hurrying toward Jonathan, Skye took a deep breath and sent up a silent prayer. *Please, God, let him be all right.* Kneeling down, she squinted, scanning the boy's silent body. She spotted one sock and pant leg saturated with blood. Carefully, slowly, she reached out and touched Jonathan on his knee.

Jonathan jumped, and Skye's nerves jumped too. The boy bolted upright, his eyes wide with panic. Scrambling backward, he pressed tightly against the dark wall of the niche.

"Jonathan, it's me!" Skye signed and then opened her arms toward the boy.

For a brief moment, Jonathan sat frozen on the spot, his eyes wide with fear. Then he broke into a smile, and with a deep, shaky breath, he reached toward Skye. Before she could respond, he threw his arms around her neck. Like a cold, wet sponge, he clung to his rescuer, embracing her as though he would never let go.

"Thank you, God!" Skye drew the boy into a bear hug, wet and cold. But at that moment, wet and cold didn't matter. Nothing mattered but Jonathan. Skye had found him, and he was safe. "Oh, Jonathan," she whispered, hugging him tighter. "You crazy kid."

Moving back, Skye looked into Jonathan's eyes. "Are you okay?" she signed.

"My ankle." The boy grimaced in pain. "I can't walk on it."

"Chad!" Skye yelled. "Bring the first-aid kit!"

"I've got it with me!" Chad yelled as he joined Skye.

Skye's gaze never drifted from Jonathan's face. "How did you get here? And how long have you been here?"

"I like water, so yesterday I rode Buddy up to the campsite," he signed. "We found this new trail leading back here. He tripped, and I fell off. I landed on my ankle. Then I crawled in here because I couldn't get back on my horse."

As Chad approached, Skye took a second look at Jonathan's leg. "The way that's swollen, it must be a bad sprain," she signed. "Or maybe it's broken!"

Tears flooded Jonathan's eyes, running in deep tracks down his dirty cheeks. "I'm sorry," he signed, crying. "I'll never do this again. I don't hate you. I'm sorry." Releasing a painful moan, he reached toward his ankle.

With a reassuring smile, Skye helped him position his injured leg. "I don't hate you either, Jonathan. I love you," she signed.

Chad handed Skye the first-aid kit. "We need to get him out of this dampness!" He was hoarse from trying to make himself heard. "You take the kit and get the blankets off our horses. I'll have to carry him out of here. Mr. Wheaten said the storms are about half an hour away. He's sending a truck and a horse trailer down to the campsite. The men should be here in about twenty minutes!"

"The campsite is partly hidden under this huge bluff!" Skye yelled. "If it rains before they get here, we can stow away under there!" She turned to Jonathan. "Chad's going to carry you back to the campsite. Okay?"

"Okay," he signed. "I'm sorry."

"I know," Skye said.

Skye carefully supported Jonathan's leg. As though the boy were a feather, Chad gently swooped him up. Still wincing in pain, Jonathan forced a smile. His eyes, searching deep into Skye's, seemed filled with a new understanding of God's love and true friendship. "I don't hate you anymore," he signed. "I love you." He pointed to both Skye and Chad.

"What did he say?" Chad asked.

"He said he loves us," Skye said.

"Tell him I love him too," Chad said.

"We love you," Skye signed. "And your parents do too. They're waiting for you at Camp Oneega."

"My father too?" Jonathan's face beamed. "My father came to camp?"

"Yes," Skye signed, "your father too."

"But he doesn't care what I do," Jonathan signed.

"Oh, yes, he does, Jonathan," Skye signed. "Both your parents are worried about you. They can't wait to see you. And when we get back, they have a surprise. A very big surprise. Don't they, Chad?"

"One he won't believe." Chad gave Skye the dimpled smile that made her heart flutter.

Skye blinked back a flood of new tears. Her whole body revived with joy, and her heart filled with brand-new emotions. "Thank you, God," she whispered as she turned to walk out. "Jonathan's not the only one who learned a lesson. Now I know what friendship and team-work really mean, with others and with you. God, you are so awesome!"

Skye followed Chad and Jonathan out of the cave, glanced back at the falls, and smiled.

A Letter to my
Keystone Stables Fans

Dear Reader,

Are you crazy about horses like I am? Are you fortunate enough to have a horse now, or are you dreaming about the day when you will have one of your very own?

I've been crazy about horses ever since I can remember. When I was a child, I lived where I couldn't have a horse. Even if I had lived in the country, my folks didn't have the money to buy me one. So, as I grew up in a small coal town in central Pennsylvania, I dreamed about horses and collected horse pictures and horse models. I drew horse pictures and wrote horse stories, and I read every horse book I could get my hands on.

For Christmas when I was ten, I received a leather-fringed western jacket and a cowgirl hat. Weather permitting, I wore them when I walked to and from school. On the way, I imagined that I was riding a gleaming white steed into a world of mountain trails and forest paths.

Occasionally, during the summer, my mother took me to a riding academy where I rode a horse for one hour at a time. I always rubbed my hands (and hard!) on my mount before we left the ranch. For the rest of the day I tried not to wash my hands so I could smell the horse and remember the great time I had. Of course, I never could sit at the dinner table without Mother first sending me to the faucet to get rid of that "awful stench."

To get my own horse, I had to wait until I grew up, married, and bought a home in the country with enough land for a barn and a pasture. Moon Doggie, my very first horse, was a handsome brown and white pinto Welsh Mountain Pony. Many other equines came to live at our place where, in later years, my husband and I also opened our hearts to foster kids who needed a caring home. Most of the kids loved the horses as much as I did.

Although owning horses and rearing foster kids are now in my past, I fondly remember my favorite steed, who has long since passed from the scene. Rex, part Quarter Horse and part Tennessee Walker, was a 14 ½ hands-high bay. Rex was the kind of horse every kid dreams about. With a smooth walking gait, he gave me a thrilling ride every time I climbed into the saddle. Yet, he was so gentle, a young child could sit confidently on his back. Rex loved sugar cubes and nuzzled my pockets to find them. When cleaning his hooves, all I had to do was touch the target leg, and he lifted his hoof into my waiting hands. Rex was my special horse, and although he died at the ripe old age of twenty-five many years ago, I still miss him.

If you have a horse now or just dream about the day when you will, I beg you to do all you can to learn how to treat with tender love and respect one of God's most beautiful creatures. Horses make wonderful pets, but they require much more attention than a dog or a cat. For their loyal devotion to you, they only ask that you love them in return with the proper food, a clean barn, and the best of care.

Rex

Although Skye and Jonathan's story that you just read is fiction, the following pages contain horse facts that any horse lover will enjoy. It is my desire that these pages will help you to either care for your own horse better now or prepare you for that moment when you'll be able to throw your arms around that one special horse of your dreams that you can call your very own.

Happy riding!
Marsha Hubler

Are You Ready to Own Your First Horse?

The most exciting moment in any horse lover's life is to look into the eyes of a horse she can call her very own. No matter how old you are when you buy your first horse, it's hard to match the thrill of climbing onto his back and taking that first ride on a woodsy trail or dusty road that winds through open fields. A well-trained mount will give you a special friendship and years of pleasure as you learn to work with him and become a confident equestrian team.

But owning a horse involves much more than hopping on his back, racing him into a lather of sweat, and putting him back in his stall until you're ready to ride him again.

If you have your own horse now, you've already realized that caring for a horse takes a great amount of time and money. Besides feeding him twice a day, you must also groom him, clean his stall, "pick" his hooves, and have a farrier (a horseshoe maker and applier) and veterinarian make regular visits.

If you don't own a horse and you are begging your parents to buy one, please realize that you can't keep the horse in your garage and just feed him grass cuttings left over from a mowed lawn. It is a sad fact that too many neglected horses have ended up in rescue shelters after well-meaning families did not know how to properly care for their steeds.

If you feel that you are ready to have your own horse, please take time to answer the following questions. If you say yes to all of them, then you are well on your way to being the proud owner of your very own mount.

1. Do you have the money to purchase:

   - the horse? (A good grade horse can start at $800. Registered breeds can run into the thousands.)
   - a saddle, pad, and bridle, and a winter blanket or raincoat? ($300+ brand new)
   - a hard hat (helmet) and riding boots? ($150+)
   - essentials such as coat and hoof conditioner, bug repellent, electric clipper and grooming kit, saddle soap, First Aid kit, and vitamins? ($150+)

2. Does your family own at least a one-stall shed or barn and at least two acres of grass (enough pasture for one horse) to provide adequate grazing for your horse during warm months? If not, do you have the money to regularly purchase quality oats and alfalfa/timothy hay, and do you have the place to store the hay? Oh, and let's not forget the constant supply of sawdust or straw you need for stall bedding!

3. Are you ready to get up early enough every day to give your horse a bucket of fresh water, feed him a coffee can full of oats and one or two sections of clean dry hay (if you have no pasture), and "muck out" the manure from the barn?

4. Every evening, are you again ready to water and feed your horse, clean the barn, groom him, and pick his hooves?

5. Will you ride him at least twice a week, weather permitting?

6. If the answer to any of the above questions is no, then does your family have the money to purchase a horse and board him at a nearby stable? (Boarding fees can run as high as a car payment. Ask your parents how much that is.)

So, there you have the bare facts about owning and caring for a horse. If you don't have your own horse yet, perhaps you'll do as I did when I was young: I read all the books I could about horses. I analyzed all the facts about the money and care needed to make a horse happy. Sad as it made me feel, I finally realized that I would have to wait until I was much older to assume such a great responsibility. And now years later, I can look back and say, "For the horse's sake, I'm very glad I did wait."

I hope you've made the decision to give your horse the best possible TLC that you can. That might mean improving his care now or waiting until you're older to get a horse of your own. Whatever you and your parents decide, please remember that the result of your efforts should be a happy horse. If that's the case, you will be happy too.

Let's Go Horse Shopping!

If you are like I was when I was younger, I dreamed of owning the most beautiful horse in the world. My dream horse, with his long-flowing mane and wavy tail dragging on the ground, would arch his neck and prance with only a touch of my hand on his withers or a gentle rub of my boot heel on his barrel. My dream horse was often different colors. Sometimes he was silvery white; other times he was jet black. He was often a pinto blend of the deepest chocolate browns, blacks, and whites. No matter what color he was, he always took me on a perfect ride, responding to my slightest commands.

When I was old enough to be responsible to care for my own steed, I already knew that the horse of my dreams was just that, the horse of my dreams. To own a prancing pure white stallion or a high-stepping coal-black mare, I would have to buy a Lipizzaner, American Saddle Horse, or an Andalusian. But those kinds of horses were either not for sale to a beginner with a tiny barn or they cost so much, I couldn't afford one. I was amazed to discover that there are about 350 different breeds of horses, and I had to look for a horse that was just right for me, possibly even a good grade horse (that means not registered) that was a safe mount. Color really didn't matter as long as the horse was healthy and gave a safe, comfortable ride. (But I'm not sure what my friends might have said if I had a purple horse. That certainly would have been a "horse of a different color!") Then I had to decide if I wanted to ride western or English style. Well, living in central Pennsylvania farm country with oodles of trails and dirt roads, the choice for me was simple: western.

I'm sure if you don't have your own horse yet, you've dreamed and thought a lot about what your first horse will be. Perhaps you've already had a horse, but now you're thinking of buying another one. What kind should you get?

Let's look at some of the breeds that are the most popular for both western and English riders today. We'll briefly trace a few breeds' roots and characteristics while you decide if that kind of horse might be the one for you. Please keep in mind that this information speaks to generalities of the breeds. If given the proper care and training, most any breeds of horses make excellent mounts as well.

Some Popular Breeds (Based on Body Confirmation)

The Arabian

Sometimes called "The China Doll of the Horse Kingdom," the Arabian is known as the most beautiful of horse breeds because of its delicate features. Although research indicates Arabians are the world's oldest and purest breed, it is not known whether they originated in Arabia. However, many Bible scholars believe that the first horse that God created in the Garden of Eden must have embodied the strength and beauty that we see in the Arabian horse of today. It is also believed that all other breeds descended from this gorgeous breed that has stamina as well as courage and intelligence.

A purebred Arabian has a height of only 14 or 15 hands, a graceful arch in his neck, and a high carriage in his tail. It is easy to identify one of these horses by examining his head. If you see a small, delicate "dish" face with a broad forehead and tiny muzzle, two ears that point inward and large eyes that are often ringed in black, you are probably looking at an Arabian. The breed comes in all colors, (including dappled and some paint), but if you run your finger against the grain of any pureblood Arabian's coat, you will see an underlying bed of black skin. Perhaps that's why whites are often called "grays."

Generally, Arabians are labeled spirited and skittish, even though they might have been well trained. If you have your heart set on buying an Arabian, make sure you first have the experience to handle a horse that, although he might be loyal, will also want to run with the wind.

The Morgan

The Morgan Horse, like a Quarter Horse (see below), can explode into a gallop for a short distance. The Morgan, with its short legs, muscles, and fox ears, also looks very much like the Quarter Horse. How can we tell the two breeds apart?

A Morgan is chunkier than a Quarter Horse, especially in his stout neck. His long, wavy tail often flows to the ground. His trot is quick and short and with such great stamina, he can trot all day long.

So where are the Morgan's roots?

The horse breed was named after Justin Morgan, a frail music teacher who lived in Vermont at the turn of the eighteenth century. Instead of receiving cash for a debt owed, Mr. Morgan was given two colts. The smallest one, which he called Figure, was an undersized dark bay with a black mane and tail. Mr. Morgan sold the one colt, but he kept Figure, which he thought was a cross between a Thoroughbred and an Arabian. Over the years, he found the horse to be strong enough to pull logs and fast enough to beat Thoroughbreds in one afternoon and eager to do it all over again the same day!

When Mr. Morgan died, his short but powerful horse was called "Justin Morgan" in honor of his owner. After that, all of Justin Morgan's foals were called Morgans. The first volume of the Morgan Horse Register was published in 1894. Since then, hundreds of thousands of Morgans have been registered.

If you go Morgan hunting, you will find the breed in any combination of blacks, browns, and whites. Don't look for a tall horse because all Morgans are between 14 and 15 hands tall, just right for beginners. If you're fortunate enough to find a well-trained Morgan, he'll give you years of pleasure whether you ask him to gallop down a country trail, pull a wagon, or learn to jump obstacles.

The Mustang

If you want a taste of America's Wild West from days gone by, then you should treat yourself to the "Wild Horse of America," the Mustang.

This 14–15 hand, stout horse has its roots from Cortez and the Spanish conquistadors from the sixteenth century.

Although the Mustang's name comes from the Spanish word, *mesteno*, which means "a stray or wild grazer," he is most well known as the horse of the Native Americans. Numerous tribes all over the western plains captured horses that had escaped from their Spanish owners and ran wild. The Native Americans immediately claimed the Mustang as a gift from their gods and showed the world that the horse was, and is, easy to train once domesticated.

It didn't take long for the white settlers to discover the versatility of the Mustang. Because of his endurance, this little horse soon became a favorite for the Pony Express, the U.S. cavalry, cattle round-ups, and caravans.

Since the 1970s, the U.S. Bureau of Land Management has stepped in to save the Mustangs from extinction. As a result, herds of Mustangs still roam freely in U.S. western plains today. At different times of the year and in different parts of the country, the Adopt-a-Horse-or-Burro Program allows horse lovers to take a Mustang or burro home for a year and train it to be a reliable mount. After the year, the eligible family can receive a permanent ownership title from the government. As of October 2007, more than 218,000 wild horses and burros have been placed into private care since the adoption program began in 1973.

If you'd like a "different" kind of horse that sometimes has a scrubby look but performs with the fire of the Arab-barb blood, then go shopping for a Mustang. You'll find him in any black, brown, or white combination and with the determination and stamina to become your best equine friend.

The Quarter Horse

There's no horse lover anywhere in the world who hasn't heard of the American Quarter Horse. In fact, the Quarter Horse is probably the most popular breed in the United States today.

But what exactly is a Quarter Horse? Is he only a quarter of a horse in size, therefore, just a pony? No, this fantastic breed isn't a quarter of anything!

The Quarter Horse originated in American colonial times in Virginia when European settlers bred their stout English workhorses with the Native Americans' Mustangs. The result? A short-legged but muscular equine with a broad head and little "fox" ears, a horse that has great strength and speed.

It didn't take long for the colonists and Native Americans to discover that their new crossbreed was the fastest piece of horseflesh in the world for a quarter of a mile. Thus, the breed was christened the American Quarter Horse and began to flourish. Besides running quick races, it also pulled wagons, canal boats, and plows. When the American West opened up, cowpokes discovered that the Quarter Horse was perfect for herding cattle and to help rope steers. Although it remained a distinct breed for over three hundred years in the U.S., the Quarter Horse was only recognized with its own studbook in 1941.

If you are looking for a reliable mount that has a comfortable trot and smooth gallop, you might want to look at some *seasoned* Quarter Horses. (That means they have been trained properly and are at least five or six years old.) They come in any color or combination of colors. Their temperament is generally friendly, yet determined to get the job done that you ask them to do.

The Shetland Pony

Many beginning riders incorrectly believe that the smaller the horse, the easier it is to control him. You might be thinking, "I'm tiny, so I need a tiny horse!" But many beginners have found out the hard way that a Shetland Pony is sometimes no piece of cake.

Shetland Ponies originated as far back as the Bronze Age in the Shetland Isles, northeast of mainland Scotland.

Research has found that they are related to the ancient Scandinavian ponies. Shetland Ponies were first used for pulling carts, carrying peat and other items, and plowing farmland. Thousands of Shetlands also worked as "pit ponies," pulling coal carts in British mines in the mid–nineteenth century. The Shetland found its way at the same time to the United States when they were imported to also work in mines.

The American Shetland Pony Club was founded in 1888 as a registry to keep the pedigrees for all the Shetlands that were being imported from Europe at that time.

Shetlands are usually only 10.2 hands or shorter. They have a small head, sometimes with a dished face, big Bambi eyes, and small ears. The original breed has a short, muscular neck, stocky bodies, and short, strong legs. Shetlands can give you a bouncy ride because of their short broad backs and deep girths. These ponies have long thick manes and tails, and in winter climates their coats of any color can grow long and fuzzy.

If you decide you'd like to own a Shetland, spend a great deal of time looking for one that is mild mannered. Because of past years of hard labor, the breed now shows a dogged determination that often translates into stubbornness. So be careful, and don't fall for that sweet, fuzzy face without riding the pony several times before you buy him. You might get a wild, crazy ride from a "shortstuff" mount that you never bargained for!

The Tennessee Walking Horse

If you buy a Tennessee Walker, get ready for a thrilling ride as smooth as running water!

The Tennessee Walking Horse finds its roots in 1886 in Tennessee, when a Standardbred (a Morgan and Standardbred trotter cross) stallion named Black Allan refused to trot; instead, he chose to amble or "walk" fast. With effortless speed comparable to other horses' trots,

Black Allan's new gait (each hoof hitting the ground at a different time) amazed the horse world. Owners of Thoroughbreds and saddle horses were quick to breed their mares to this delightful new "rocking-horse" stud, and the Tennessee Walker was on its way to becoming one of the most popular breeds in the world. In just a few short years, the Walker became the favorite mount of not only circuit-riding preachers and plantation owners, but ladies riding sidesaddle as well.

Today the Walker, which comes in any black, brown, or white color or combination, is a versatile horse and is comfortable when ridden English or Western. He is usually 15 to 17 hands tall and has a long neck and sloping shoulders. His head is large but refined, and he has small ears. Because he has a short back, his running walk, for which he is known, comes naturally.

If you go shopping for a Tennesee Walker, you will find a horse that is usually mild mannered yet raring to go. Although most walkers are big and you might need a stepstool to climb on one, you will be amazed at how smooth his walk and rocking-horse canter is. In fact, you might have trouble making yourself get off!

Some Popular Breeds (Based on Body Color)

The Appaloosa

French cave paintings thousands of years old have "spotted" horses among its subjects, ancient China had labeled their spotted horses as "heavenly," and Persians have called their spotted steeds "sacred." Yet the spotted Appaloosa breed that we know today is believed to have originated in the northwestern Native Americans tribe called the Nez Perce in the seventeenth century.

When colonists expanded the United States territory westward, they found a unique people who lived near the Palouse River (which runs from north central Idaho to the Snake River in southeast Washington State). The

Nez Perce Indian tribe had bred a unique horse—red or blue roans with white spots on the rump. Fascinated, the colonists called the beautiful breed *palousey*, which means "the stream of the green meadows." Gradually, the name changed to *Appaloosa*.

The Nez Perce people lost most of their horses following the end of the Nez Perce War in 1877, and the breed started to decline for several decades. However, a small number of dedicated Appaloosa lovers kept the breed alive. Finally, a breed registry was formed in 1938. The Appaloosa was named the official state horse of Idaho in 1975.

If you decide to buy an Appaloosa, you'll own one of the most popular breeds in the United States today. It is best known as a stock horse used in a number of western riding events, but it's also seen in many other types of equestrian contests as well. So if you would like to ride English or Western, or want to show your horse or ride him on a mountain trail, an Appaloosa could be just the horse for you.

Appaloosas can be any solid base color, but the gorgeous blanket of spots that sometimes cover the entire horse identifies the special breed. Those spotted markings are not the same as pintos or the "dapple grays" and some other horse colors. For a horse to be registered as a pureblood Appaloosa, it also has to have striped hooves, white outer coat (sclera) encircling its brown or blue eyes, and mottled (spotted) skin around the eyes and lips. The Appaloosa is one of the few breeds to have skin mottling, and so this characteristic is a surefire way of identifying a true member of the breed.

In 1983, the Appaloosa Horse Club in America decided to limit the crossbreeding of Appaloosas to only three main confirmation breeds: the Arabian, the American Quarter Horse, and the Thoroughbred. Thus, the Appaloosa color breed also became a true confirmation breed as well.

If you want your neighbors to turn their heads your way when you ride past, then look for a well-trained Appaloosa. Most registered "Apps" are 15 hands or shorter but are full of muscle and loaded with spots. Sometimes, though, it takes several years for an Appaloosa's coat to mature to its full color. So if it's color you're looking for, shop for a seasoned App!

The Pinto

The American Pinto breed has its origins in the wild Mustang of the western plains. The seventeenth and eighteenth century Native Americans bred color into their "ponies," using them for warhorses and prizing those with the richest colors. When the "Westward Ho" pioneers captured wild Mustangs with flashy colors, they bred them to all different breeds of European stock horses. Thus, the Pinto has emerged as a color breed, which includes all different body shapes and sizes today.

The Pinto Horse Association of America was formed in 1956, although the bloodlines of many Pintos can be traced three or four generations before then. The association doesn't register Appaloosas, draft breeds, or horses with mule roots or characteristics. Today more than 100,000 Pintos are registered throughout the U.S., Canada, Europe, and Asia.

Pintos have a dark background with random patches of white and have two predominant color patterns:

1. Tobiano (Toe-bee-ah'-no) Pintos are white with large spots of brown or black color. Spots can cover much of the head, chest, flank, and rump, often including the tail. Legs are generally white, which makes the horse look like he's white with flowing spots of color. The white usually crosses the center of the back of the horse.

2. Overo (O-vair'-o) Pintos are colored horses with jagged white markings that originate on the animal's side or belly and spread toward the neck, tail, legs, and back. The deep, rich browns or blacks appear to frame the white. Thus, Overos often have dark backs and dark legs. Horses with bald or white faces are often Overos. Their splashy white markings on the rest of their body make round, lacy patterns.

Perhaps you've heard the term *paint* and wonder if that kind of horse is the same as a Pinto. Well, amazingly, the two are different breeds! A true Paint horse (registered by the American Paint Horse Association) must be bred from pureblood Paints, Quarter Horses, or Thoroughbreds. The difference in eligibility between the two registries has to do with the bloodlines of the horse, not its color or pattern.

So if you're shopping for a flashy mount and you don't care about a specific body type of horse, then set your sites on a Pinto or Paint. You might just find a well-trained registered or grade horse that has the crazy colors you've been dreaming about for a very long time!

The Palomino

No other color of horse will turn heads his way than the gorgeous golden Palomino. While the average person thinks the ideal color for a Palomino is like a shiny gold coin, the Palomino breed's registry allows all kinds of coat colors as long as the mane and tail are silvery white. A white blaze can be on the face but can't extend beyond the eyes. The Palomino can also have white stockings, but the white can't extend beyond the knees. Colors of Palominos can range from a deep, dark chocolate to an almost-white cremello. As far as body confirmation, four breeds are strongly represented in crossbreeding with the

Palomino today: the American Saddlebred, Tennessee Walker, Morgan, and Quarter Horse.

No one is sure where the Palomino came from, but it is believed that the horse came from Spain. An old legend says that Isabella, queen of Spain in the late fifteenth century, loved her golden horses so much she sent one stallion and five mares across the Atlantic to start thriving in the New World. Eventually those six horses lived in what is now Texas and New Mexico, where Native Americans captured the horses' offspring and incorporated them into their daily lives. From those six horses came all the Palominos in the United States, which proves how adaptable the breed is in different climates.

Today you can find Palominos all over the world and involved in all kinds of settings from jumping to ranching to rodeos. One of their most popular venues is pleasing crowds in parades, namely the Tournament of Roses Parade in Pasadena, California, every New Year's Day.

Perhaps you've dreamed of owning a horse that you could be proud of whether you are trail riding on a dirt road, showing in a western pleasure class, or strutting to the beat of a band in a parade. If that's the case, then the Palomino is the horse for you!

If you're shopping for the best in bloodlines, look for a horse that has a double registry! With papers that show the proper bloodlines, an Appaloosa Quarter Horse can be double registered. Perhaps you'd like a palomino Morgan or a pinto Tennessee Walker?

Who Can Ride a Horse?

As you have read this book about Skye, Morgan, and some of the other children with special needs, perhaps you could identify with one in particular. Do you have what society calls a handicap or disability? Do you use a wheelchair? Do you have any friends who are blind or have autism? Do you or your friends with special needs believe that none of you could ever ride a horse?

Although Keystone Stables is a fictitious place, there are real ranches and camps that connect horses with children just like Skye and Morgan, Sooze in book two, Tanya in book three, Jonathan in book four, Katie in book five, Joey in book six, and Wanda in book seven. That special kind of treatment and interaction has a long complicated name called Equine Facilitated Psychotherapy (EFP.)

EFP might include handling and grooming the horse, lunging, riding, or driving a horse-drawn cart. In an EFP program, a licensed mental health professional works together with a certified horse handler. Sometimes one EFP person can have the credentials for both. Whatever the case, the professionals are dedicated to helping both the child and the horse learn to work together as a team.

Children with autism benefit greatly because of therapeutic riding. Sometimes a child who has never been able to speak or "connect" with another person, even a parent, will bond with a horse in such a way that the child learns to relate to other people or starts to talk.

An author friend has told me of some of her family members who've had experience with horses and autistic children. They tell a story about a mute eight-year-old boy who was taking therapeutic treatment. One day as he was riding a well-trained mount that knew just what to do, the horse stopped for no reason and refused to budge. The leader said, "Walk on" and pulled on the halter, but the horse wouldn't move. The sidewalkers (people who help the child balance in the saddle) all did the same thing with the same result. Finally, the little boy who was still sitting on the horse shouted, "Walk on, Horsie!" The horse immediately obeyed.

So the good news for some horse-loving children who have serious health issues is that they might be able to work with horses. Many kids like Morgan, who has cerebral palsy, and blind Katie (book five) actually can learn to ride! That's because all over the world, people who love horses and children have started therapy riding academies to teach children with special needs how to ride and/or care for a horse. Highly trained horses and special equipment like high-backed saddles with Velcro strips on the fenders make it safe for kids with special needs to become skilled equestrians and thus learn to work with their own handicaps as they never have been able to do before!

A Word about Horse Whispering

If you are constantly reading about horses and know a lot about them, you probably have heard of horse whispering, something that many horse behaviorists do today to train horses. This training process is much different than what the majority of horsemen did several decades ago.

We've all read Wild West stories or seen movies in which the cowpoke "broke" a wild horse by climbing on his back and hanging on while the poor horse bucked until he was so exhausted he could hardly stand. What that type of training did was break the horse's spirit, and the horse learned to obey out of fear. Many "bronco busters" from the past also used whips, ropes, sharp spurs, and painful bits to make the horses respond, which they did only to avoid the pain the trainers caused.

Thankfully, the way many horses become reliable mounts has changed dramatically. Today many horses are trained, not broken. The trainer "communicates" with the horse using herd language. Thus, the horse bonds with his trainer quickly, looks to that person as his herd leader, and is ready to obey every command.

Thanks to Monty Roberts, the "man who listens to horses," and other professional horse whispering trainers like him, most raw or green horses (those that are just learning to respond to tack and a rider) are no longer broken.

Horses are now trained to accept the tack and rider in a short time with proven methods of horse whispering. Usually working in a round pen, the trainer begins by making large movements and noise as a predator would, encouraging the horse to run away. The trainer then gives the horse the choice to flee or bond. Through body language, the trainer asks the horse, "Will you choose me to be your herd leader and follow me?"

Often the horse responds with predictable herd behavior by twitching an ear toward his trainer then by lowering his head and licking to display an element of trust. The trainer mocks the horse's passive body language, turns his back on the horse, and, without eye contact, invites him to come closer. The bonding occurs when the horse chooses to be with the human and walks toward the trainer, thus accepting his leadership and protection.

Horse whispering has become one of the most acceptable, reliable, and humane ways to train horses. Today we have multitudes of rider-and-horse teams that have bonded in such a special way, both the rider and the horse enjoy each other's company. So when you're talking to your friends about horses, always remember to say the horses have been trained, not broken. The word *broken* is part of the horse's past and should remain there forever.

Bible Verses about Horses

Do you know there are about 150 verses in the Bible that include the word *horse*? It seems to me that if God mentioned horses so many times in the Bible, then he is very fond of one of his most beautiful creatures.

Some special verses about horses in the Bible make any horse lover want to shout. Look at this exciting passage from the book of Revelation that tells us about a wonderful time in the future:

"I saw heaven standing open and there before me was a white horse, whose rider is called Faithful and True. With justice he judges and makes war. His eyes are like blazing fire, and on his head are many crowns. He has a name written on him that no one knows but he himself. He is dressed in a robe dipped in blood, and his name is the Word of God. The armies of heaven were following him riding on white horses and dressed in fine linen, white and clean" (Revelation 19:11–14).

The rider who is faithful and true is the Lord Jesus Christ. The armies of heaven on white horses who follow Jesus are those who have accepted him as their Lord and Savior. I've accepted Christ, so I know that some day I'll get to ride a white horse in heaven. Do you think he will be a Lipizzaner, an Andalusian, or an Arabian? Maybe it will be a special new breed of white horses that God is preparing just for that special time.

Perhaps you never realized that there are horses in heaven. Perhaps you never thought about how you could go to heaven when you die. You can try to be as good as gold, but the Bible says that to go to heaven, you must ask Jesus to forgive your sins. Verses to think about: "For all have sinned and fall short of the glory of God" (Romans 3:23); "For God so loved the world that he gave his one and only son, that whoever believes in him shall not perish but have eternal life (John 3:16); "For everyone who calls on the name of the Lord will be saved" (Romans 10:13).

Do you want to be part of Jesus' cavalry in heaven some day? Have you ever asked Jesus to forgive your sins and make you ready for heaven? If you've never done so, please ask Jesus to save your soul today.

As I'm riding my prancing white steed with his long wavy mane and tail dragging to the ground, I'll be looking for you!

Glossary of Gaits

Gait – A gait is the manner of movement; the way a horse goes.

There are four natural or major gaits most horses use: walk, trot, canter, and gallop.

Walk – In the walk, the slowest gait, hooves strike the ground in a four-beat order: right hind hoof, right fore (or front) hoof, left hind hoof, left fore hoof.

Trot – In the trot, hooves strike the ground in diagonals in a one-two beat: right hind and left forefeet together, left hind and right forefeet together.

Canter – The canter is a three-beat gait containing an instant during which all four hooves are off the ground. The foreleg that lands last is called the *lead* leg and seems to point in the direction of the canter.

Gallop – The gallop is the fastest gait. If fast enough, it's a four-beat gait, with each hoof landing separately: right hind hoof, left hind hoof just before right fore hoof, left fore hoof.

Other gaits come naturally to certain breeds or are developed through careful breeding.

Running walk–This smooth gait comes naturally to the Tennessee walking horse. The horse glides between a walk and a trot.

Pace–A two-beat gait, similar to a trot. But instead of legs pairing in diagonals as in the trot, fore and hind legs on one side move together, giving a swaying action.

Slow gait–Four beats, but with swaying from side to side and a prancing effect. The slow gait is one of the gaits used by five-gaited saddle horses. Some call this pace the *stepping pace* or *amble*.

Amble–A slow, easy gait, much like the pace.

Rack–One of the five gaits of the five-gaited American saddle horse, it's a fancy, fast walk. This four-beat gait is faster than the trot and is very hard on the horse.

Jog–A jog is a slow trot, sometimes called a *dogtrot*.

Lope–A slow, easygoing canter, usually referring to a western gait on a horse ridden with loose reins.

Fox trot–An easy gait of short steps in which the horse basically walks in front and trots behind. It's a smooth gait, great for long-distance riding and characteristic of the Missouri fox trotter.

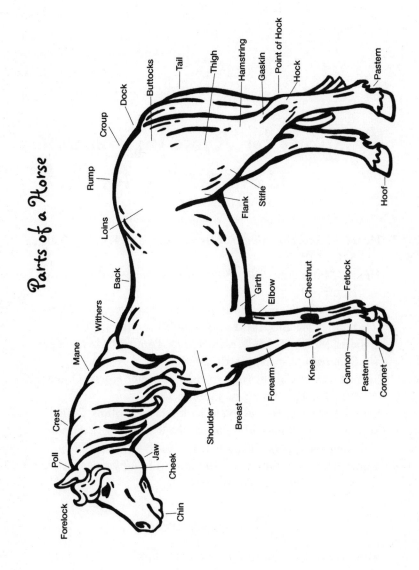

Parts of a Horse

Resources for Horse Information Contained in this Book

Henry, Marguerite. *Album of Horses*. Chicago: Rand McNally & Co., 1952.

Henry, Marguerite. *All About Horses*. New York: Random House, 1967.

Jeffery, Laura. *Horses: How to Choose and Care for a Horse*. Berkley Heights, NJ: Enslow Publishers, Inc., 2004.

Roberts, Monty. *The Horses in My Life*. Pomfret, VT: Trafalgar Square Publishers, North, 2004.

Self, Margaret Cabell. *How to Buy the Right Horse*. Omaha, NE: The Farnam Horse Library, 1971.

Simon, Seymour. *Horses*. New York: HarperCollins, 2006.

Sutton, Felix. *Horses of America*. New York: G.P. Putnam's Sons, New York City, 1964.

Ulmer, Mike. *H is for Horse: An Equestrian Alphabet*. Chelsea, MI: Sleeping Bear Press, 2004.

Online resources

http://www.appaloosayouth.com/index.html
http://www.shetlandminiature.com/kids.asp
http://www.twhbea.com/youth/youthHome.aspx